THE RYDER CODE

Lawrence J. Epstein

Fig Hollow

CHAPTER ONE

Spring 1943
New York City

The man in the doorway stood as still as the two marble lions at the New York Public Library. He was a stocky man who had the look of someone who enjoyed combat. He steadied himself like a soldier ready to pounce. He had a calmness that I had seen before in former fighters who had formed a friendship with death.

He wore a light blue jacket although the night was still brimming with heat. He was hiding a weapon. His skin was red, maybe from some disease.

I had seen professional killers with kinder faces.

Then his eyes slowly scanned the diner.

I was seated in the back booth of the all-night diner, which I used as an office. The man spotted me and his eyes stopped moving.

I keep a revolver under my hat on my right side. The Derringer is behind the sugar on the booth's table top. I casually moved my hat directly next to me.

Gertie, the waitress who doubled as my secretary, got behind the counter. She had a shotgun there.

Someone else came into the diner.

I stared. Then I blinked and stared again.

It was a nun. I am a skilled detective and could tell this because she was wearing a habit.

Unless it was a disguise.

She was not a frightening figure. The nun was small with a substantial build. She had the eyes of an eagle looking for prey. She was old and frail.

The man who looked like a killer nodded toward me. Since it was four in the morning and only a few people were in the place, the nun could easily figure out I was the one being singled out.

I put my right hand under my hat and moved the revolver under the table. I didn't usually deal with nuns, real or fake, and I wasn't taking any chances.

The nun didn't smile. She didn't look angry. Her face was weathered. She looked as though she made a hobby of collecting lines in that face.

The one who looked like a killer was three steps behind her but not reaching for any weapon.

The nun arrived at my table.

I could see she was too old to be wandering New York's dark streets at night.

"You are perhaps Mr. Ryder, the private detective?"

Her voice had a rasp to it. It was soft but filled with authority.

"I am for the right person."

No smile. Focus. Concentration. She was serious. A comedian would go broke trying to make this nun laugh.

"May I sit down?"

"Send your bodyguard outside."

"I can't. My bodyguard is assigned to protect me. We are not here to hurt you or threaten you."

"He's threatening just standing there."

The nun nodded.

"That is his job. I am glad he is doing it well."

"If he moves, I shoot you."

"Yes. You have a weapon under the table aimed at

me. But you didn't shoot. So we can talk."

I didn't move my hand.

"Sit down. You have two minutes."

"I'll need more than that, Mr. Ryder. But I'll start and you can see what you want to do."

"Go ahead."

The nun nodded.

I still had no idea what was going on.

She cleared her throat and continued. "Some ground rules. I am going to tell you the truth. The center of that truth is that I need you. If the truth bothers you at any point, tell me and I will work harder to convince you to listen to me."

"Who are you?"

"You may call me Sister Grace. I come from another place. I am the leader of a secret group made up of nuns, priests, and some friends."

That's when I thought she might be crazy.

"You'll excuse me, Sister. I'm good at recognizing people who are not tethered tightly to reality."

I leaned forward. "In case you didn't know, we're sitting in Greenwich Village, New York. You do understand that? You haven't escaped from a hospital have you? You're not just telling me some tale that lives only in your mind?"

"I'm quite tied to the real world. I'm painfully tied to it. I'm here for a meeting with friends later this morning. Important friends. I'm staying at the Hotel Fourteen at 14 East 60th Street."

"What's in the basement of the hotel?"

"I hear it called the Copacabana. I believe it is some kind of nightclub. I have never been there. I do not have time for such nonsense."

"Maybe you would benefit from some nonsense in your life."

She shrugged. "I assure you I wouldn't."

"All right. Let's say you are who you say you are. What do you want from me?"

"Your friend Mr. Rosenblatt said you could be completely trusted."

I relaxed a bit.

"You should have started with that. His mother taught me right from wrong. What she taught me has guided my life."

The nun began to interest me.

She was evaluating me as much as I was her. "But you are not Catholic."

"Trust me. Neither is Mr. Rosenblatt. I am not anything and I'm everything."

"This sounds like a riddle told by a Zen Buddhist."

"Maybe I'm that too. You come from a spiritual world. I come from the steps of an orphanage. I was left there. I don't know exactly what I am."

"I know what you are. You are an outsider. Maybe then you will be able to help me." The nun paused. "Mr. Ryder, you can read my face. I am a serious person. A very serious person. I don't joke around. I don't understand the jokes on the radio."

"You didn't tell me what you wanted."

"Can I have a cup of coffee?"

I signaled to Gertie. She came over with the coffee pot, turned over the two cups on the table, and poured us very hot drinks.

The nun sipped. She took out a bar of chocolate from somewhere in her habit, unwrapped it, and chewed a piece before going back to the coffee.

She was nervous. She didn't trust me. And what she wanted to say was important, too important to tell to a man she didn't know and didn't trust.

But from the fact that she was here, she had no choice.

The nun sighed.

I took my hand off my weapon.

"So," she said, "Let us begin."

CHAPTER TWO

"Mr. Rosenblatt said you know much about what the Nazis are doing to the Jews. The whole world is slowly learning the truth."

"I know enough."

Sister Grace nodded.

"Good. The People of the Holy Book are a broken people. Many of the Jews of Europe have been killed. Many have lost hope."

She paused and looked down.

She was getting ready to tell me the secret she carried.

"Mr. Ryder, there are Jewish children all over Europe without families, without protection. There is a group to which I belong that seeks to find these children and protect them."

"You hide them from the Nazis?"

She nodded.

"We hide them in convents. We teach them prayers to fool the Nazis. We give them new names. We try to get them smuggled out and bring them where we can."

She paused and sipped the coffee again.

"This is very difficult because the countries don't want them. Imagine. Lost little children. Many of them desperate and hungry orphans. And nobody will take them in. Mr. Ryder, do you know that America does not even fill its legal quota which is horribly, tragically small? If I weren't a nun I would say these countries are complicit in the death of the children."

"But you are a nun."

"Yes. Sometimes I wish I weren't, so I could yell out. I'd feel better. But for now we…we have to use bribes sometimes. We have to lie. We have to hide. But we lie only to the Nazis. We do whatever we have to do to get those children to safety."

She gave out a deep sigh. I don't think I had ever heard a nun sigh before. Hers was deep from her center. It was an echo of the world's pain.

"It is a simple matter in some ways, Mr. Ryder. The more money we have the more children we can help."

I looked into her eyes.

"I'm obviously very sympathetic to your efforts Sister," I said, "Beyond that you are brave, heroic, and deeply admirable. But I have no great amount of money. I'm afraid there's not much I can do."

"My meeting later is with men who have money. We need so much money. To survive as a group, Mr. Ryder. To keep working. Mr. Rosenblatt told me you were very smart. He said if I even told one little lie you would know that. I see he was right. But not one word I have said to you is a lie or an exaggeration."

"What happens in the convents?"

She stared at me.

"Some believe we should baptize the children."

She crossed herself. "Some believe we should turn them over to the Nazis."

"But most have a deep faith in the Lord. It is our duty to save the life of every child we can. Our group is out to save Jewish children as Jewish. We do not baptize them. We rescue them. We hide them in the convents. We feed and clothe them. Sometimes it is laughable, Mr.

Ryder. We try to teach them about their Jewish heritage. You'd be surprised how much we learn when we do this. I have become friends with rabbis and Jewish teachers. I have learned much from them."

"I admire all of you who rescue these children. But I still don't see where I fit in."

The nun was ready. The pitch was coming.

"You are a detective."

"I prefer to call myself a fixer."

"But this is just what we need, someone to fix the problem we have."

"Tell me about your problem, Sister Grace."

"There is a man who lives in New York. For the moment I won't reveal his name."

"I take it this man has money."

"He does, and he is sympathetic to our cause."

"But..."

"But, he wants something in return for giving us the money. Something we can't give him, but I believe it is something you can."

"What does he want?"

"His daughter was killed three months ago. He had a heart attack in reaction. He has recovered but he is very sad all the time. I visited him. He understands when I talk in code about what the money will be used for."

She was delaying answering me directly, so I said, "The police did not solve the crime?"

"No, Mr. Ryder."

"And you think I can?"

"I don't think you can. You have to. This rich man has told me to my face that when the killer is found and is dead or in jail this wealthy man will donate three million dollars to us. You can't imagine what that would mean to the children. In truth, I'm not sure I can even imagine."

We sat in silence for a moment.

"Mr. Ryder, I became a nun because I wanted a quiet spiritual life within. I wanted to withdraw from the pains and terrors of the world. I wanted to focus on prayer and service."

"And then the Nazis came."

She nodded. "Indeed. And this quiet little girl within me one day saw Nazi soldiers kicking a man on the ground. I saw one of them shaving his beard while the other soldiers laughed. I saw them take their rifle butts and hit him in the face. I saw blood flowing out.

"I didn't know what I was doing, Mr. Ryder, but it was at that very moment that I vowed that I would do whatever I could.

"And then one day I saw children crying. I took them to our convent. I...there was an argument, but they stayed. I have never stopped and I never will."

She looked down.

"Once I found a little boy and asked him his name. He answered 'Dirty Jew.' Mr. Ryder I cannot stop. The Lord would never forgive me."

She had a fire in every vein and spoke to me with the sound that could have come from an ancient prophet.

"I am asking for your help Mr. Ryder in letting us rescue the children. You say you are a fixer. Find the killers of the daughter of this man who can help us."

"Sister Grace, I meant what I said. I'm extremely sympathetic to your cause. But the police in New York are extraordinarily good. If they could not find the killers, I don't think I will be able to do so."

"Mr. Rosenblatt said you help people in trouble

and do so sometimes without telling them. You are a good man. He said that you've solved crimes no one else could. He called you a miracle worker. Mr. Ryder, we need a miracle worker. I believe in you. You can't be a believer alive today and not believe in miracles. We are not going to give up now."

"Who's the man who lost his daughter?"

"His name is Adam Lonigan. He is a jeweler. A very successful one obviously."

Sister Grace took a napkin and wrote down an address and phone number.

"There are two more issues, Mr. Ryder. Serious ones, I'm afraid."

Her eyes never left mine. This was one tough fighter.

"First, Mr. Ryder, I have an obligation to tell you that the Nazis are aware of our efforts, and they need to stop me. They have sent an agent to the United States. The agent's goal is to kill me here. If that happens, the focus will not be on Europe. The Nazis will claim America is a dangerous and degenerate place."

"Who is this agent?"

"I don't know his name. I do know his code name. It is Tristan. Mr. Ryder, you are putting yourself in danger by helping me. This Tristan may go after you."

"I appreciate the warning, Sister Grace. And I take this person seriously. But we are living in the middle of history. I am called to do what is right, even in the face of danger."

She looked at me and nodded.

"Good. And the final matter. You are a detective, Mr. Ryder. It is how you make your living. People pay you to discover hidden information. My last question is how much will you charge us for your services in finding the killers?"

"Sister Grace, look at me. Do you seriously think I would charge you money to help innocent children escape history's greatest monster? There is no charge."

Sister Grace sat still for a moment.

Then she said, "So you are saying yes, right Mr. Ryder?"

"I am saying yes. I had a heart problem and they won't let me fight in the war. I want to very much. I have a daydream of putting my hands around Hitler's throat. Maybe I can fight now."

I took the napkin.

Sister Grace stuck out her hand.

I shook it.

I looked at her.

She looked up and said, "What do you believe in, Mr. Ryder? This is very important to me. I am, as I said, a believing Catholic. I pray to the Holy Mother. I obey the sacraments. I sing the hymns. My voice is not so good. One friend said I didn't sing the hymns so much as murder them. I go to confession. I want to know what you believe in."

"I believe we get the meaning of our lives from the accumulation of moral choices we make. I deeply admire your moral choices, Sister. But I don't pray."

"Yes you do, Mr. Ryder. You pray with your conscience. You become a partner with God with your good deeds."

We looked at each other for a moment.

She stood up.

So did I.

The bodyguard still looked scary.

I watched as they left the diner.

Gertie came over.

"That doesn't happen every night in here, Ryder."

"We're lucky if it happens once in a lifetime, Gertie."

"I take it she gave you a job."

"No, Gertie. She gave me a mission."

CHAPTER THREE

Detective Simon Hill was sitting opposite me in the diner. Working homicides in New York City gnaws on your sanity. Hill had once come to me about his missing sister and I had, to a point, helped him. We had worked together, sometimes uncomfortably, since then.

His hair was thinning. His skin had acquired a shade of elephant gray. He had lost the last bit of his faith in people, which hadn't been that great to begin with. Losing faith in people is what happens if you see enough corpses and hear enough stories about what people can do to each other.

Hill felt guilty about every murder he couldn't solve. He told me the victims cried out to him in his dreams and begged him not to stop looking. He didn't drown his guilt in scotch the way others did. He just lived with it. The pain rattled around in his brain, jumping out at unsuspected moments.

Gertie came over and brought us both hamburgers. Hill buried his in ketchup. Then he used more ketchup on his potatoes.

"It's therapy," he said when he saw me stare at him for pouring so much from the ketchup bottle. "It pours like blood. I figure if I stare at it and control it and eat it, the real stuff won't bother me as much as it does."

"My guess is you never studied psychology," I said. "You might want to see somebody about that ketchup theory."

He took several bites of the hamburger and ate some potatoes. Then he looked up at me.

"You may not believe this Ryder, but the New York City police department in general and the boys in Homicide in particular don't like it when you go looking at an open case. It's true we didn't close the Lonigan case. But your taking it is doing nothing less than mocking us, saying we're not good enough to find the killers, but you are."

He ate some more and then said, "And I take it as personal that you won't say why you're doing this. So everyone asked me first to say you should drop it. They also said you should drop dead and other unkind words but I'm leaving all of that out."

"I can't drop it, Detective."

He nodded. "You give stubborn a bad name."

"Did you get the report?"

"Sure. I mean I love to steal police files for someone outside the force."

He pushed the folder across to me.

"Tell me what happened before I dig into this," I said. "Please."

"The deal still stands, right? If through some blind bit of luck you find the killers, you tell me and I arrest them?"

"That's the deal. Unless they're dead."

"Don't go around saying things like that. I like them alive. The citizens of the city used to put up with dead horses lying in the street. They really didn't like those and they really, really don't like seeing dead bodies as they walk to work."

"I'll do my best. I know it all took place in a bakery."

"It did. The dead woman you asked about, Rebecca Lonigan, was at the bakery store, the one on St. Marks, the kosher one, Benny's."

"I know it. Benny makes good chocolate cakes. I assume that isn't in the report."

Hill ignored me. "Anyway, she's in there buying cakes and cookies. She's buying them for school children. She has a list of those kids with birthdays. The teachers give her a list of kids who can't afford this stuff. She buys it…I mean bought it, took it to the school, and the teacher had a little party for the kid. Everyone's happy. She's like you, Ryder. The teachers wanted to introduce her to the class, but she never let them. Kind but anonymous."

"What happened?"

"What happened was two guys came in waving weapons. Benny was behind the counter. Miss Lonigan was one of two customers."

Hill took some more bites. Gertie brought him a big slice of apple pie with vanilla ice cream on top of it.

He took some of that.

"Woman named Mrs. Della Benson was the other customer. Then the two guys come into the bakery. They had on fedoras and red bandanas over their faces. They asked Benny for the money. He opened the cash register and gave them the week's total, about two thousand dollars. It looked like that's all they wanted and then were going to leave. Benny had his hands up. Nobody was going to shoot them."

"So what went wrong?"

"No one knows. They're about to leave and they start shooting. They hit Benny and both women."

"What was the order of shots?"

Hill sat there.

"You're not as dumb as you look. Which is a great relief. What we know we learned from Benny, the only survivor. Maybe he's telling the truth, maybe he's not. But he said the Benson woman got hit first, then the one you asked about, Miss Lonigan, and then Benny."

"Isn't that strange? Wouldn't they go after Benny first? He's a man. Maybe he has a weapon behind the counter."

Hill shrugged. "I considered that, and I don't think the order matters. If Benny remembered it correctly and if he's telling the truth, no one was putting up a fight. They could have shot Benny first and then the women. It wouldn't have made a difference."

"But Benny survived."

"He did. The women were killed immediately, but he was hit in the shoulder."

I leaned forward. "That's a lot of money for a week in a bakery."

"We know that."

"So you must have thought what I did. Maybe it was some guys Benny knew. He gets shot to make it look authentic. There's really like sixty dollars taken, but he reports a couple of thousand and gets it back from the insurance company."

"We did look at that. You know Benny, though."

I nodded. "He's honest. He wouldn't do it. And besides if he did arrange it, there was no reason to shoot anyone. They would have needed customers as witnesses, and so they would have wanted the women to be alive."

Hill said, "We reached the same conclusion. But that just adds to the confusion. Who robs a bakery? A bank sure. But a bakery? And you kill people?"

"You guys still working on it?"

Hill looked at me. "Officially, the police never stop looking for a vicious killer. We're here to protect the public."

"And unofficially?"

"We can't keep up with new killings. There's not much time or energy for cases we've already looked at."

Gertie refreshed my coffee cup, and I took a few sips.

"You have any suggestions, Detective?"

"I don't know, Ryder. Maybe start with Benny."

"I will, and I have to investigate the two women, but there's someone I have to see first."

"And that would be?"

"An important person."

"Thanks for your close cooperation. There's nothing special in all those reports."

Hill lowered his head.

"I guess I've got to get back to my wife."

"You two doing okay?" His wife had walked out on him a couple of months earlier, but they got back together.

"I look at my wife in a realistic way. She's a punishment from God."

"It must be fun at your dinner table."

"I'm here aren't I?"

He stood up slowly and began to walk to the door.

I watched Hill go.

Gertie came over. "He looks like a very unhappy man."

I nodded. "He can't leave his job and doing his job is killing him."

"You know, Ryder, sometimes you talk in a very strange way."

I went home and got some sleep.

I had a big appointment at ten o'clock.

CHAPTER FOUR

I was up early the next morning. That wasn't because I was alert or enthusiastic or good at my work. It was because I couldn't sleep. I looked at sleep as my mortal enemy.

I had some toast and coffee.

Then I called Vinny.

"I'm surprised you're up Ryder."

"No one is more surprised than I am. I have an appointment."

"Be careful or someone is going to confuse you with a professional."

"Not if they see me at work."

"What do you need?"

"You remember that robbery in the bakery? Benny's. Three months ago. Two women killed."

"I remember. Three months isn't that long ago and I won't be senile for at least two more months."

"You hear anything about the boys who did it?"

"I heard they were professional or acted professional. The shooter knew how to shoot."

"Isn't that strange, Vinny? I mean I can see two kids doing it, not two people who knew their way around weapons. It was a bakery not a poker game."

"I know. I can't tell you it's a fact. I can just tell you what I heard."

"Professional like this is what they do for a living or professional like they really planned it out and made sure nothing went wrong."

"No idea, Ryder. You want a guess?"

"Sure."

"They were from out of town. Somebody would have heard more if they were from here."

"But Vinny, if that's true it's even stranger. Why should someone bring in people from out of town to rob a bakery? I'm sorry, but the fact that it was a bakery really gets to me."

"You're the detective Ryder. I'm a simple man."

"Yeah. A simple guy who knows every hit man, thief, and mobster in the City."

"I told you what I know."

"Dig deeper, Vinny. Find out what you can about those two guys. And the two women."

"Usual rates?"

"Double for good information gotten quickly."

"Give me a real incentive"

"Triple if you don't try to push me any more."

"Triple it is. I'll get on it."

Then I called Ruth Draper. Ruth worked in the diner at night. Her uncle owned the place. It didn't need another waitress but that's what uncles can do. She was a good person. I gave her assignments now and then. Her husband had been killed in the war and she had never gotten over it.

I understood what Ruth was going through. My wife, Maggie, was dead for a couple of years, and I still thought that I saw her sometimes on the streets. Maybe going into a store or rushing to the next street.

"Hi, Mr. Ryder."

"Hi, Ruth. Quick question. Do you want an assignment?"

"I hope it's dangerous."

"Sorry. One day."

"You keep saying that."

"And one day I'll be right, Ruth. Just not today."

A sigh.

"Whatever you need."

"The mark of a great detective."

"I don't just want to be a detective. I want to be a fixer like you Mr. Ryder."

"You have a pencil, Ruth?"

"What kind of waitress would I be if I didn't have one?"

"All right. Put this down. There were two women killed a few months ago in a bakery. Rebecca Lonigan and Della Benson. Check all the papers. Talk to the reporters. Do a background check. Find out all you can about these two women and about Benny who owns the bakery where they were shot."

"I notice you didn't ask me to check about the killers."

"I'm having Vinny do that."

"He may have been one of them."

"No," I said, "Vinny stays away from the violence and he always has an alibi when he sends someone out to do a killing."

"All right, Mr. Ryder. Can I ask you a question?"

"Sure."

"Gertie said Detective Hill was in last night. Did he come then because it was my night off?"

"No. He came because that's when I needed him."

Ruth and Detective Hill had just begun a romance when Hill's wife returned to their home and they decided to try to make their marriage work. Ruth had never healed from the hurt. She said it was like her husband dying again.

"Mr. Ryder, you never lie to me. Is he happy?"

"He's a homicide detective. If he were happy, I'd worry about him."

She thanked me and hung up. I thought I heard her gently weeping.

I shaved twice. I put on a dark blue suit, my most expensive one. I picked out a powder blue tie. It was supposed to make me look serious. I checked myself in the mirror. Maybe Mr. Lonigan would tip me with jewels from his store.

I decided to arrive in a cab. I don't like it at all but appearances matter in my business.

Park Avenue is a bit out of my league. I saw people who had been walking their dogs for so long they began to look like each other. I saw a radio singer I knew a little bit smiling as he walked by. He didn't nod at me. Then I went up to the door.

A man answered. I suppose he was technically the butler, but if so he was a butler who could have gone into wrestling instead.

"Good morning, sir. May I help you?"

It was an accent from 91st Street not someplace in London. The image was ruined for me.

"Yes," I said. "My name is Jack Ryder. I have an appointment with Mr. Lonigan."

The butler nodded and let me into the hall. By hall I mean a room that was larger than any room I had ever been in. It could have been modeled after the Taj Mahal for all I knew.

"I apologize sir, but I'm obliged to check you for weapons. Mr. Lonigan is very concerned about his security."

"As he should be. But he lets you carry."

"I am part of the household."

"Look. I have a thirty-eight on my left side in a hol-ster. If Mr. Lonigan doesn't like that, I'll understand and leave. But nobody takes it from me. Nobody."

"I'm sure he'll understand sir. He's most anxious to meet you."

"Good."

I followed the butler. The rooms I saw looked like Lonigan had seen them in a palace and then copied the design and gotten replicas of the contents.

Lonigan was behind a desk in the library. He was talking on the telephone. I didn't know if he had read the books or just had them for show.

The butler had me sit in a chair opposite Lonigan.

Then Lonigan hung up the phone, stared at me for a second, and said, "Sister Grace promised me you would find my daughter's killer. Is that right?"

I cleared my throat.

CHAPTER FIVE

"I'm going to do my best," I said. "Promises are for politicians and religious leaders and con men. They aren't for the honest detective."

"Mr. Ryder, she was my only child. I'm a widower. You know I already had a heart attack. If there is no justice for my child, there is no life for me. I will curl up and die. I apologize for piling emotional pressure on you. I just want you to realize the stakes for me."

He took a sip of water. It was a cruelly hot day.

"The police have failed me. The private detectives I hired have failed me. You understand my skepticism in the midst of my desperately clinging to Sister Grace's promise."

Lonigan cleared his throat. "Mr. Ryder, I have agreed to have you investigate simply because everyone else has failed. I have gotten a quick overview of your character. I must express my astonishment at how many people were willing to talk about you. You won't be surprised, Mr. Ryder, that certain people used very harsh language indeed in talking about you. They called you a cold-blooded killer, a man with no respect for society or rules, a broken man who consorts with the lowest forms of humanity."

He stopped to extend his lower lip outwards.

"And yet your successes are unmistakable. Very impressive I must say. One of my contacts had an interesting contribution. One of the good parts of having money is that I know people in a wide variety of ways. This contact I mention said you had on several occasions helped the FBI. I found that dissonant with the other parts of your personality that I had put together. Do you wish to comment?"

"I do, Mr. Lonigan. And here is my comment. It is my policy not to discuss my clients or people I help. I assume you approve of such a policy."

Lonigan nodded. "I do. Still, the FBI. Knowing that will give me some reassurance that you're not just some hoodlum looking to get some money from Sister Grace or me."

"She did not offer me any money and I did not ask for any. It is my contribution to her efforts."

He stared at me. "I also have to consider that you agreed to get to know my business, the layout of my store and diamond collection with the intention of transferring some of my diamond collection to yourself."

"Did anyone speak to you to say I was a thief?"

"No, they didn't. They said they wouldn't cross you. That you go right through the stop signs of life. That it is not a good idea to get in your way. These are characteristics of a man I find valuable. So I will reveal myself a bit to you."

He leaned forward to make sure I was focused just on him. He was a tall man with gray hair at the sides of his head and no hair on top. He was overweight. His eyes were moist. I'm not sure if the moisture came from tears or sweat.

"I have been the most grateful of American citizens. The diamond business has been good to me. Very good. I have a big house, an expensive car, prominent paintings on my walls that should bring comfort but don't. You understand?"

"I understand grief but not as deeply as you do, Mr. Lonigan."

"All my diamonds and all my money have become comically trivial in my life. People tell me time is a great healer. So far it has failed me. A specialist I went to told me the killers will be caught. But that if they're not I should have faith that somehow the world will find a way to punish them. That is too abstract for me. You may say I am bloodthirsty. I seek revenge. To the world I say I seek justice, but in bed at night I am all alone with a God I don't believe in. Then I seethe with thoughts of revenge."

"May I bring up a delicate subject?"

"I'd be disappointed in you if you didn't."

"Sister Grace told me you would donate a large sum, a very large sum, to help her organization."

"That is correct. The children she helps break my heart. They need a place to stay, a safe place, a home. We have to help them rebuild their lives. If I were younger and stronger I would go to Europe and help in the rescue."

I nodded.

"I'm going to speak bluntly, Mr. Lonigan. Sister Grace and her people need that money. It's not fair to hold it ransom to finding your daughter's killers. It is unlikely that I will be any more successful than the police. I know them. They are most efficient."

"But they are overwhelmed by the numbers of people killed. They are restricted by the law in terms of the actions they can take. They have no emotional stake in finding these killers." His voice was a mixture of anguish and desperation. He took another drink.

"All of that is true," I said, "but you haven't told me why you don't give the money now. I promise I will look for the murderers as hard as I can and Sister Grace will be able to work with the money now."

He leaned back. "They do need the money now. You are right. So then find the killers, and I will give the money. I have always found rewards make excellent incentives."

"So do the millions of little children who cry out for your help. I don't need an incentive."

"I can't change who I am, Mr. Ryder."

"What was your daughter like, Mr. Lonigan?"

"It will sound like an exaggeration, as though my memory and love have distorted reality. But Rebecca was truly an exceptional human being. She was much nicer than I am. When on the rare occasion we argued it was over how much money she was donating to hospitals, schools, orphanages, and the poor directly. If anyone deserved to be a saint Rebecca was that person."

"May I have a look at her room? Surely you have preserved it exactly as she left it."

He tilted his head to one side. An eye closed.

"It's a sacred place, Mr. Ryder. The killing was, as the police told me, a matter of her being in the wrong place at the wrong time. It wasn't about her as a person. I can't see what you can accomplish by prying into her private life."

"Mr. Lonigan, of course I respect your sense of privacy as well as Rebecca's. It's just the way I work. I check every corner of a life. We don't really know why she was shot. There was no reason to shoot her or the other woman who was a customer. I start at the beginning and I keep going."

"And if I refuse, will you stop your investigation?"

"Of course not. But I will say to you directly that

if you get in the way of my methods you are hindering my ability to find the killers. If you're all right with that, then by all means call your butler and have me escorted out."

"People don't talk to me like that."

"I'm not people."

"I'm uncomfortable with your looking in her room."

"Then be uncomfortable."

He nodded.

"Come on. I'll show you her room. It's upstairs. Please do not disturb it. It is an important part of my memory."

We went to her room. It was large with a bed lined with toy animals. Lonigan left me alone in the room. I scanned around looking at the remains of a lost life.

A normal man would have cried.

I walked over to the closet, got down on my hands and knees, and looked on the floor. Then I checked under the mattress all the way around the bed and looked beneath the bed itself.

The bureau was smaller than I expected. I went through the clothes and jewelry in its drawers.

I had saved the desk for last. I sat down, trying to be her. Where would I keep my diary so my father wouldn't see it? I imagined he was not the kind of person who would spy on his daughter, but I imagined her as cautious so she could be entirely honest in the diary's pages. If there was a diary.

The middle drawer on the right side was locked. I took out my collection of skeleton keys. The third one opened the lock.

There were papers. I reached under them and

found what I was looking for.

I put the diary in my inside jacket pocket. There was a slight bulge but not one I thought that would arouse Mr. Lonigan's concern. I continued to look through the desk.

Twenty minutes later I found my way downstairs, thanked Mr. Lonigan, promised to keep him informed, repeated my suggestion that he donate money now, and left.

I headed right home.

I was planning to read the diary and make another call.

When I got there, I saw Gloria sitting on the front stoop. Her long blonde hair was damp with perspiration. She didn't see me immediately because her beautiful face was in her hands. Her sobbing was controlled, but I could hear its pain.

I said hello in a soft voice.

"Oh, Mr. Ryder, please can I talk to you? I'm so upset."

"Come on, Gloria. We need to get you out of this heat."

She stood up, took my arm, and we walked inside.

CHAPTER SIX

Gloria had once worked for Vinny. Her general job was to attract men. That was easy with the excess of bouncy blonde hair and a body that carried its own extraordinary allures for men to stare at it. Gloria knew how to dress, how to walk, and how to talk to men. She could have been a very successful flirting coach.

I paid Vinny to let her go. That makes me sound virtuous, but I used her the same way Vinny did, although I just used her looks. I didn't force her into any relationships with men. This, I suppose, makes me half-moral, but only just that.

For several years I had been trying to help her make her way back into a normal life. I knew she was currently working as a waitress at a fancy French restaurant in midtown.

I got both of us glasses of lemonade. She took time out from weeping long enough to have a long drink. Then she put the glass down, looked at me, and said, "You have no idea what it is like to be me, Mr. Ryder. You're really lucky."

"I'm sorry, Gloria. You're right. I have no idea what it's like to be anybody else including you. Take a few deep breaths and tell me what the trouble is."

She nodded, did some breathing, took another drink, almost finishing the lemonade, and said, "I got fired."

"I've been in the restaurant, Gloria. You're a wonderful waitress. I'm a 'don't make a single mistake' kind of person with myself, and that was the kind of waitress you were."

"Thank you, Mr. Ryder. I think I need to wait twenty years and then go back to waitressing or any other job for that matter."

"Tell me the story, Gloria."

"Could I have some more lemonade, Mr. Ryder?"

I nodded, got up, and refilled her glass.

After another long drink, she said, "The owner said I had to do him a favor if I wanted to keep the job. And I had to do the favor every week."

"What's the owner's name?"

"Claude Martine."

"I'll have a chat with Mr. Martine, Gloria."

"Oh, don't do that, Mr. Ryder. I just want to forget it all. I'll be fine after a week of crying."

I got up, went into another room where my desk stood, and took out ten hundred dollar bills.

I returned and gave the money to Gloria. "This is for you to get by until you get another job."

"I can't take this, Mr. Ryder. I didn't earn it."

"You did, Gloria. It's a bonus for all the excellent work you've done for me."

"I could use it."

"It's yours. What kind of job can you look for?"

"I've worked in dress shops, flower shops, a hotel once. I'm not trained for anything. I can't type well or I'd be a secretary. I'd like to be a legal secretary. That sounds like fun. And you get to meet lawyers."

I didn't want to tell her that some of the lawyers I knew made Claude Martine seem shy.

"I'd offer you work, Gloria, but you know the kind

of people I meet and the sort of work I'd need."

"You mean being a dumb and available blonde."

I was so embarrassed at her accurate summary that all I could do was nod.

"I'll take it, Mr. Ryder. You treat me good. You never would do what Mr. Martine did. You're honest about what you want. And you don't make me do anything disgusting with those men you meet." She paused and looked down. "I'm ashamed to admit it, but I like the attention. I like men telling me how beautiful I am and how they want to invite me for a week in Paris. I like their words but not what they want to do."

"The problem is I can't offer you enough work, Gloria. Just from time to time. Let me think about it."

"I'm a real good cook. That was part of what Mr. Martine said. That I could work in the kitchen as part of his deal."

"That helps."

"You made me feel much better, Mr. Ryder."

"Thanks."

She put her arms around my neck and kissed me. The perfume was intoxicating. But I didn't kiss her back.

"Your late wife must have been a special woman, Mr. Ryder. I can tell you she was the luckiest woman in the world to have a man like you."

"Sure. Every woman wants a private eye walking through dark streets on darker nights and dealing with killers, gamblers who haven't been honest since they were babies if then, and people who enjoy crushing anyone who gets in their way. No, Gloria, a husband with a normal life is better for a woman, any woman, including you, maybe especially you."

"I'd take you any time, Mr. Ryder."

With that, she got up and left.

I had a peanut butter and jelly sandwich and sat down.

Phone calls came first.

I called Vinny.

"I don't have any information yet, Ryder. Don't be impatient."

"I'm giving you additional work. This will be easier and faster. You can give it to one of your boys in training and still make good bucks."

"You're speaking my language, Ryder. What is it?"

I told him the name and location of the restaurant. "The owner is a guy named Claude Martine. I need background information. I want to blackmail him and I need damaging information."

"Why don't you use Gloria to get some intimate photos? She does still work for you, doesn't she?"

"No. And even if she did I would never have her do that."

"So what information do you want?"

"If I knew I'd get it. You need to look. Can you do this?"

"You pay me enough and I can give birth to triplets."

"That will not be necessary."

We jokingly insulted each other a bit and hung up.

Then I called Tommy. He's my body man. He owns a run-down funeral home, but he has access to information about anyone's death. He also carts away dead bodies that are inconveniently lying down where I shot them. Once in a while, I even need a dead body. Tommy complains, but I think he likes what he does.

Tommy was the one who told me that he's come to

believe that the dead can hear us. He has talks with them. He says in private, when no one is around, that the dead cry blood. They are struggling to get back to life. They are trying to remind us to embrace life when we are living because one day we will be gone and can't become alive again.

"Ryder? It's been too long. Either shoot more people or shoot straighter."

"I'm calling you Tommy to see if you need a helper in your business."

"What kind of helper?"

"The girl Gloria I sometimes use."

"Are you kidding? She would make the dead bodies I deal with sit up and try to kiss her. She's not a funeral kind of girl, Ryder. A dancer maybe. I know you like her or I'd make another suggestion."

"No chance, Tommy?"

"None. You want anything else?"

I had a thought that came suddenly to my head.

"Yeah. Thanks for asking. You remember those two women killed in Benny's bakery?"

"Vaguely."

I reminded him of the incident.

"Okay," Tommy said, "So what's that got to do with me?"

"This may be a dark road leading to a blind alley, but I want to find out about those two women."

"Ryder. They were shot. I'm guessing even you could figure out the cause of death."

"You can get more information from a body than that they have a bullet in them. Maybe there were more bullets. Maybe one was pregnant. Maybe one was dying."

"I'll see what I can do. I don't like to disappoint you

about the dame Gloria or the two stiffs. Half-price on this Ryder."

"You're going soft, Tommy."

"Don't tell no one. Anyway, lots of people died this week. I'm filled up. Got some guys shipped back from overseas. They were stuck there for a while. That's the army. Anyway, I'm sorry."

"Thanks Tommy."

I finally sat down, picked up a copy of Rebecca Lonigan's diary, moved a bit so I could put my feet up, and I began to read.

CHAPTER SEVEN

"I am lost. I am my father's daughter. And that's good because he loves me. By love he means he gives me money, way more money than I need. He cares about me, too much to understand that I sometimes need to be free. I need to stop thinking about how I do will affect him. I feel like a bird kept in a beautiful cage, able to eat seeds whenever I want but unable to fly. Or maybe I'm a painting unable to move out of my frame."

I started turning pages of the diary. The same basic ideas were repeated over and over in different ways. What interested me most was the nature of her rebellion.

Rebecca Lonigan helped the poor and the powerless. She gave money and food. She gave her time and her energy. And she did it all anonymously.

"Yesterday, I went to Benny's Bakery. I talked to him. I had seen him giving free cookies and cupcakes to kids who stared in the shop's windows but looked too poor to come inside. Benny would run around the counter and go outside. He'd talk to the kids and then invite them inside and give them something. Sometimes it was bread because they had none at home. Sometimes it was a product to put on bread. Sometimes it was one of those cookies he keeps in his window that everyone wants, the cookie with jelly in the window and sugar all around it on the cookie."

I felt Rebecca and I were somehow spiritually connected. The more I read the more pain I felt.

She was no longer just a victim. Her spirit screamed out for justice, to be remembered and that spirit to be made whole again.

Rebecca didn't do a lot of thinking about the world. She didn't wonder why some people were good and others not. She didn't write about politics or the unspeakable brutality of the Nazis. Her world was small but vital to her. She reminded me of Emily Dickinson with cookies instead of poems.

And then, suddenly, I was overwhelmed with a sense of not belonging. I had opened her diary when I had no right to do so. I did get a sense of the woman. I felt a push inside me to find her killers.

There was no place in her diary that indicated a dark side. I had been looking for her visits to an opium den on the Lower East Side or a gambling establishment she visited regularly where she and a lover drank away the evening. I wanted someplace where she could meet those who lived outside the law, people who thought she knew too much or saw what she should not have seen. Someone with a motive to kill her.

But I could not find anyone like that.

Motives to kill are strange. We are all so dark inside with a castle of feelings and thoughts surrounded by a moat that is not passable by other human beings.

Maybe she had visits to places she did not put in the diary. Perhaps she thought her father was so controlling that he felt it acceptable to search for and read her diary and so she left what he would think of as the inappropriate out of there.

Maybe she had a friend who seemed nice but inside an inner castle had hostile thoughts about Rebecca. She was pretty. She was innocent. To men I knew, she screamed out that she was a victim.

Maybe some friend she had was like me, believing he was alone in life and not revealing himself to others.

I stopped reading for a second.

Then I was back in the real world holding Rebecca's diary that recorded her inner world. I held the diary with the same reverence a believer holds the Bible. And, like the Bible, I used that diary as a book to make a vow.

I promised Rebecca, wherever she was, and I promised myself as I sat there that I would bring her killers to justice.

CHAPTER EIGHT

Benny Oppenheim was small. He had over- sampled the cakes and cookies in his bakery. He had a lot of hair for someone his age. His glasses were thick but the eyes behind them were alert.

"It's been a while, Mr. Ryder."

"Too long Benny. How are you feeling?"

He shrugged. "I may have to close. It's not a disaster. My wife wants me to retire. My feet want me to retire. But what am I going to do, Mr. Ryder? Sit around all day and listen to the radio? And I ain't feeling so good. I only got it in the shoulder. So everyone tells me I'm lucky. They ain't never been shot in the shoulder, I can tell you that."

"You got a minute to sit and talk?"

"I probably got an hour. All my regular customers, they're old. They're scared. They're too scared of coming in here. They're afraid of getting shot. In their heads they know that's ridiculous, but fear is a funny thing. You feel it and it takes you over. So yeah. You sit down. I'll bring over some coffee for us both and a nice piece of chocolate cake. I remember you like that."

I laughed.

"Benny, that's why you were always so successful. You know your customers."

He nodded. "That I do."

I sat down. It only took him a couple of minutes and he brought over the coffee and two pieces of cake along with forks.

"Eat first. Then we talk."

I wasn't about to argue. The coffee had a flavor that made it go down smoothly. The frosting on the cake melted in my mouth.

"You like?" he asked.

"It's only a little better than Heaven, Benny."

He smiled.

"Why you really here, Mr. Ryder?"

"One of the women who got shot, Benny. Her name was Rebecca Lonigan."

"Yeah. A pretty kid. Those momzers. They should die a thousand painful deaths."

"Rebecca's father wants me to find the two killers. I want to find them."

"I told the police all I knew, Mr. Ryder. You should check with them."

"I will Benny."

"You want to hypnotize me? I seen that once on stage. I don't know whether it was true."

"No, Benny. I just want you to think hard. Do you mind going over it again?"

"Truth is, it gets me upset, Mr. Ryder. But if it will help get those boys, sure."

"Okay. First of all, you told the police the men shot the other woman first and then Rebecca and then you."

"Yeah. I do remember that. I was surprised. But it all happened too fast for an old man. Truth is, I might not have remembered that part right. I know they shot the women before they shot me. But I'm not one hundred percent sure they shot the other one first."

"But you think so?"

"Yeah."

"Close your eyes, Benny."

"You gonna steal my piece of cake?"

"It's possible. But I'll try to resist."

He shut his eyes.

"Take a few deep breaths. Try to relax."

"I ain't too good at relaxing, Mr. Ryder. I got a business to run."

"Just do your best."

I waited fifteen seconds.

"Now look at those women. Who fell first?"

"It was the other woman. Then it was maybe five seconds later and this Rebecca lady collapsed. She let out a little scream. No. Maybe half a scream."

"You're doing great Benny. Keep your eyes closed and in your mind's eye picture the two men."

"Yeah. Okay."

"Tall, short?"

Benny squeezed his eyes tighter.

"They was both about the same size, average. They both wore hats and a bandana so I couldn't see their face."

"All right let's concentrate on what you did see. Were they white?"

"Yeah. Definitely."

"Did you see the color of their eyes?"

Benny shook his head.

"No. They were too far away. And my eyes ain't the best they've ever been."

"Any scars?"

"The same, Mr. Ryder. I couldn't see if they had any marks on their faces."

"Any markings on their clothes?"

"This is frustrating. No, I did see something. Their clothes were…"

"Were what, Benny?"

"The clothes looked like they didn't belong in New York?"

"What do you mean?"

"I don't know Mr. Ryder. It's just a feeling. Maybe I'm wrong. Maybe I just know my neighborhood, but them clothes looked...they looked like maybe a farmer would wear them. It was just a feeling as I say. I can't put my finger on it."

"All right. That's important. When they spoke did they have an accent? Maybe one that also didn't sound like they came from New York?"

Benny shook his head. "Only one spoke. It was like he was in charge. His voice was deep, but I didn't hear no accent. I couldn't have really, though, because all he said was that I should give him my money. I think he knew that I had a week's cash on hand, so maybe somebody who knew the store told him."

"Who might do that?"

"I don't know. I have a kid who helps me. But I know the boy's family for ten years. I saw the kid grow up. A real good kid. He goes to the museum to look at the dinosaurs. I know people, Mr. Ryder. That's my job. This is a good boy."

"All right. Were their hands shaking?"

"That's a funny question. One guy's was, but the guy in charge, his hands were steady."

"And did both do the shooting, or just the guy in charge?'

"I...I'm not sure now."

He shook his head.

"I'm sorry. I'd be a terrible cop."

"That's fine, Benny. You're doing great."

"Yeah, sure."

"Is there anything else you noticed about them?"

Benny shook his head. Then he shut his eyes again. They snapped open after a few seconds.

"What if I give you bad information? Like I said they was average size. What if they was tall?"

"You do your best."

"Yeah. But I'm the only witness."

"You want to say something, Benny. But you're not sure about it."

He was silent.

"Benny, listen. Right or wrong any impressions you had will be helpful."

"All right, but I could be wrong."

"Go ahead."

"When they was leaving, Mr. Ryder I thought I saw one of them, the one we're calling the leader, walking out."

"Good, Benny. What about his walking out?"

"I thought the leader had a slight limp."

I leaned forward.

"Are you sure Benny?"

He shook his head.

"I'm not sure at all. Between how fast it was and my nerves and bad eyesight, I'm not sure there was two men. Maybe I was seeing double."

"I doubt that, Benny. Go back to the leader who may or may not have had a limp. Did he have any kind of cane or walking stick?"

"Not that I saw."

The door opened and two customers came into the store.

Benny stood up. "I'm sorry, Mr. Ryder. You got out

more from inside of me than I thought was there. I've got to take care of my customers now."

"Thanks, Benny," I said.

I finished the coffee and cake.

It was too hot to do much walking, so I went to a park and sat in the shade. It was still hot, but I could at least think.

It was time to go home and make some lists. I would lose track if I didn't have those lists.

I didn't realize I was so tired, and I collapsed on the couch as soon as I got home.

Vinny called to wake me up.

"I got some information on your two women," he said. "I'm not done, but this will get you started."

I sat up, grabbed a pen and paper and walked over to my desk.

I was awake now.

"Okay, Vinny. Let's have it."

CHAPTER NINE

"Who do you want first, the Benson woman or the Lonigan woman?"

"Rebecca Lonigan."

"All right. Some of this is in the papers, but you should hear it as part of the background. A nice girl, Ryder. Twenty-two. Imagine that. She comes from a wealthy family. But you know that. I assume they hired you. She was an only child. The family must be going crazy."

He cleared his throat.

"You're a good customer always, Ryder, so I put some extra men on it. There's almost nothing worth telling you. She lived at home. She didn't drink. As I said, she was kind, helped people. We didn't come across anyone with a grudge. At first it looks like a wrong place at the wrong time kind of death."

"How about not at first? You said there was 'almost nothing' you thought I needed to hear. Tell me what's in that 'almost.'"

"It took some money."

"Who did you bribe? A cop?"

"No. A girl who worked in the father's store. Sold jewelry. That's painful isn't it? You're a poor kid and all day you stand around pearls and diamonds and rubies. And people who have too much come in and buy those rubies and all you can do is watch."

"So she was the right kind of person to bribe?"

"That she was, Ryder."

"What did she have to say about Rebecca?"

"It came from girl talk. There was a hidden side to Lonigan."

"Which was?"

"She had a boyfriend."

"Ah. You know his name?"

"No. The girl from the store didn't know it. She said Lonigan kept it from her father because the boyfriend wasn't Catholic and the old man was picky about that. I don't understand that, do you Ryder? I mean you find love who cares what he is?"

"Romance is not something I know about, Vinny."

"But you loved Maggie. I know that."

"I understand me. I don't understand other people."

"Oh. Anyway, this guy the boyfriend is tall, thin. The girl in the store thinks he didn't have much money."

"You know how to find him Vinny?"

"No idea. They broke up maybe two weeks before the shooting. That sounded like a good start to me."

"And me too, Vinny. You have more about him?"

"Nope. You got to begin your detecting. At least I gave you a guy to look for."

"One more question, Vinny. Did this girl in the store say what the boyfriend was like?"

"You mean did he have a temper? Was he angry about the break-up? Did he want to get even?"

"You have answers to any of those questions, Vinny?"

"Not a one. The girl saw the boyfriend exactly once and didn't talk to him or the Lonigan girl. But the time she saw him Lonigan and the boyfriend seemed to be fighting. Not yelling, mind you but not exchanging the soft sounds of love either."

"What do you know about the soft sounds of love, Vinny?"

"I heard girls like it. After that I'm lost."

"You did well."

"It's a start. We'll keep looking, but you're smarter than my boys. You should go looking."

"What about Della Benson? Anything on her?"

"She was thirty-two, lived in the neighborhood. Her husband is in the Army. In the infantry. Fought some serious battles. Got himself shot. He's in some hospital over there recovering. Sounded pretty bad. He made it through. But..."

He paused, making me almost beg him to continue.

"I bribed a neighbor of Mrs. Benson. Sweet woman." I could picture Vinny smiling.

"What did the neighbor say?"

"She said she heard when he comes back they are getting divorced."

"Is that true?"

"I can't check with every lawyer in Manhattan. I don't know what they were supposed to do when he returned."

"Where was he when Mrs. Benson died in the bakery?"

"As I said. In the hospital. Somewhere in England I think. This I double-checked. He was nowhere around New York. Too bad. That supposed divorce from his wife made him interesting."

"All right. I guess I'll have to check both women. Thanks, Vinny."

"You know how to thank me."

“Start a tab. You still have to get me information about Claude Martine, the restaurant owner.”

“Why don’t you just rough him up a bit? Or I’ll get a couple of guys to do it. The way my boys go about it, you’ll get any information you want.”

“We’ll go soft for now, Vinny.”

“You’re going to owe me a bundle, Ryder. I like that.”

“I’m sure you do, Vinny. Stay in touch.”

“I ain’t leaving my money’s side.”

We hung up.

I re-read Rebecca’s diary. There was no mention, not even a hint of a boyfriend.

But there were three mentions of a restaurant she liked to go to. Maybe the boyfriend took her there.

I never minded investigating a restaurant.

They always had coffee.

I checked the phone book. The restaurant Rebecca went to was on Fifth Avenue.

I was tired. I needed some sleep. I wanted to walk to the diner later, when it was night.

I would go to the restaurant the next day when I was fresh. I hoped there was a lot to learn there.

CHAPTER TEN

I fell asleep sitting up in the chair. I was surprised that I didn't fall off.

I started walking early.

First I went to a clothing store on West 4th Street. It was owned by a man who was supposedly Chinese. He was really Japanese and named Mr. Sawatari. No one would have gone to a Japanese store while the War kept going. Once he had slipped and told a customer that he was Korean. He always had to remember that when that customer came in, Mr. Sawatari couldn't claim to be Chinese.

"Ah, Mr. Ryder. You look like you could use a new suit."

"One day. I'll only come here to get one."

He bowed.

Then our ritual began. I handed him a good deal of money.

He bowed again.

We had agreed that when I gave him money he was not to charge the poorest people in the neighborhood. They came into the shop mostly to have their old clothes repaired. They could not even afford a new shirt. Sometimes Mr. Sawatari would tell them clothes had been donated and give them free shirts or pants or suits. He told me he especially smiled when he could give suits to young boys and fancy dresses to young girls.

I left and began walking. I went over to MacDougal

Alley with the last gas street lamps left in the City. Then I wandered over to 133-139 MacDougal Street. I had seen two plays by Eugene O'Neill produced there by The Provincetown Players.

My feet had found a comfortable rhythm and kept on going.

There were soldiers still in uniform returning from Europe. Once I met one waiting for a bus. He told me he had been a combat medic who had been reassigned to go to Japan to fight. He got back from Europe to a base in the United States. He wondered whether it would be different to fight the Japanese. I told him I didn't know. We said good-bye. I'm not sure why, but I thought about him from time to time. I wondered if he would survive the war.

I saw the diner ahead.

Ruth Draper was working alongside Gertie. Ruth ran up to me and said she wanted the honor of leading me to her booth. I told her it wasn't too much of an honor, but that I would appreciate it.

She led me to the back booth. As I sat down she said, "I got some stories about Benny and the two women who got killed. Do you want me to show you what I've got?"

"Right after you get me some coffee and some chicken with vegetables."

"You. Vegetables. There's a disconnect there, Mr. Ryder."

"The sauce Gertie cooks them in makes them edible. Otherwise if I saw a vegetable on my plate I'd get up and run screaming from the diner."

Ruth was kind enough to laugh. She went behind the counter to get a folder, came back, and sat down.

"There's not much Mr. Ryder."

She showed me the articles about the robbery. A couple of articles were about the victims. There was one follow-up article just about the two women who had been killed.

"Thanks, Ruth. I'll keep these."

"Can't I do something more dangerous now? You promised Mr. Ryder."

"If anything happened to you I could never forgive myself. Plus Gertie would stab me with a steak knife and your uncle wouldn't allow me to come back to the diner."

"How am I going to get to be a fixer like you, Mr. Ryder, if I just get articles from the papers?'

"Slowly, Ruth. Very slowly. But I'll see what I can do."

"What are going to do next?"

"I'm going to a restaurant Rebecca Lonigan used to visit. I want to see if anyone remembers her with a boyfriend."

"None of the articles mentions a boyfriend."

"There may not be one. Or if there is he may be unimportant."

"Or he may be one of the killers. That's it, Mr. Ryder. She broke up with him and he got angry. So he recruited a friend and they went there. They killed her and had to try to kill the witnesses so they wouldn't go to jail."

"That's a big stretch from where we are, Ruth."

"Wait. Can I go to the restaurant with you? I might be able to talk to a waitress. I mean I am a waitress myself. We talk the same language. They might say things about a boyfriend to me that they wouldn't say to you."

Ruth was clearly right, but I thought she was getting deeper into the case and I didn't know where it would end. An instinct told me to say no to her, but there was also the nagging feeling that it would be a waitress who had the best chance of remembering any boyfriend.

"All right, Ruth. I'm going tomorrow. Meet me at one o'clock there." I gave her the address. "But for now your adventures with this case stop there. You have to promise me that."

"I very reluctantly promise."

I got my chicken and vegetables and slowly ate them. I stared over at Ruth. Tommy and Vinny were used to sudden violence and death. They were used to people who would knife you for fifty cents. Ruth was an innocent. I couldn't shake the feeling that I needed to stop her from doing any more.

Then Gertie played "My Funny Valentine" on the jukebox and the world seemed much calmer. I focused on the eating and let go of the dark world of my life.

CHAPTER ELEVEN

My conscience is my shadow. It followed me as I went to the restaurant Rebecca Lonigan visited frequently. I relied on my conscience to whisper truths to me, to explode in indignation when I was tempted to wander off the right path, and, maybe, even to tell me when I had gone right. It rarely did the latter.

Ruth was waiting for me. She was sitting on a bench in the shade reading a book. I noticed that Ruth read a lot.

"Hi," I said going up to her. Sometimes I'm so original.

"Mr. Ryder, you're right on time. That's a very good habit."

"You hungry?" I asked, ignoring her compliment. She wasn't, after all, my conscience.

"We're not here to eat, Mr. Ryder. We have information to get. You can't ask questions if you're chewing."

"I think I've created a detecting monster."

Ruth smiled. It was a nice smile. She was in her early thirties, a couple of years younger than I was, but when she smiled she looked more like an eager teenager.

We went inside. We were brought to a table. It was a clean restaurant and looked well-organized. Rebecca wouldn't have wanted to go to a place that was splashy and expensive. She wanted nice but not a place where the rich went to congratulate themselves on having so much money.

A waitress came over.

"We're working on the air conditioning. When it's this hot outside we have trouble making it comfortable in here."

"Oh it's fine," Ruth said. "You have a nice smile."

"Aren't you nice yourself?"

"I'm a waitress like you. I know what the life is like. Let me tell you, I've had some scary people as customers."

The waitress laughed. "We should swap stories. Too bad we can't take pictures." The waitress looked at me.

"If your man wasn't here I'd ask you how many times you've been pinched."

"He's not my man. We just know each other. He comes in a lot at the diner where I work as a waitress. And the answer to your question about how many times I've been pinched is I've lost count."

I hoped Ruth just wanted to get friendly and that it wasn't true that so many men had touched her inappropriately. I feared that it was all too true.

The waitress laughed again. It wasn't a phony laugh. "So what would you like?"

I ordered a well-done hamburger.

Ruth said to the waitress, "You have a recommendation?"

"Try the tuna sandwich. The owner gets a good buy. His brother-in-law is at a fish market."

Ruth nodded.

"I'll have it then. I thank you. Even better, my stomach thanks you."

The waitress went away.

"Oh, you're good," I said to her. "I should be taking

notes."

"It's waitress to waitress Mr. Ryder. That's why I asked to come here."

The food came. I thought Ruth might ask about Rebecca Lonigan then, but she didn't. I could have prompted her, but I thought she was doing better than I could have so I decided to let her go at her own pace.

We ate the food. We talked about the diner. Ruth said she had gone on a few dates, but she couldn't stop herself from comparing the dates to her late husband who had been killed in the war and when she did the comparisons the dates seemed like pale and empty men.

The waitress came over to ask about dessert.

Before she answered, Ruth said, "Hey you seem like a perceptive person. My friend here is a reporter. Show her the picture Mr. Bell."

It took me a fraction of a second to respond. I wondered what I'd be like when I got really old. I pulled out a picture of Rebecca.

"This is a sad story and my friend has to write about her. He heard she used to come in here. You recognize her maybe?"

The waitress took the picture and looked at it.

"Yeah, sure. She came in here a lot. Always gave me a good tip. It's funny isn't it? I remember customers by how much of a tip they gave. Some people, they order the same food every time they come in and then I remember, oh, he's the steak and potatoes guy, something like that."

"Did she order a regular meal?"

The waitress shook her head. "That I can't recall."

"My friend Mr. Bell here is looking to interview people who knew her. She ever come in with somebody maybe more than once?"

"I wouldn't always remember something like that. But when you ask, yes, there was a young man she came in with quite a few times. Actually I only served them a few times but I saw them at other tables."

"Oh, Mr. Bell would love to contact him. Any idea of his name?"

The waitress put her pencil between her teeth as she thought.

Then she shook her head.

"I could be wrong. I think she called him Peter once. But I'm not sure."

"Do you remember what he looked like?"

The waitress gave a half giggle. "That I do. Real good-looking. Black hair. Very nice blue eyes. I mean you could get lost in those eyes. They were like a pool and you could dive in. Sorry. I notice eyes. That's how I'll know who's the right man for me. I'll want to fall into his eyes."

"Anything else about him?"

"Just a minute. I'll ask Janine. She had them as more regular customers. She also noticed his eyes. Janine likes to look at good-looking men."

The waitress took a step away, stopped, and turned back.

"I totally forgot. While I'm gone, can I get you some dessert?"

We both ordered Boston Cream Pie.

The waitress smiled again. "Do you know it's really a cake and not a pie?"

We both shook our heads.

"I studied desserts once. I ate more than I learned."

"Was it really created in Boston?" This was going to be my contribution to the conversation.

"Oh sure. The Parker House. Sometime in the middle of the 19ᵗʰ century. It's been around a long time. I used to know more. I do know that it's good here."

"That's what's most important," I said. I must have dazzled her with my conversational skills.

When the waitress left, I said, "No joke, Ruth. You are really good at this. People like you. You know how to put them at ease. You don't waste time. And you ask the right questions."

"Why, Mr. Ryder, thank you. I've been watching and listening to you."

The waitress was back in a few minutes.

"Janine doesn't know anything about the girl. I told you she's all about the boys. His name is Peter. I was right about that. He works at the Museum of Modern Art. He kept talking about an exhibit in February and March. Realists and some other group that I forget. Peter is arranging it and was really excited. He was writing the press release. At least that's what Janine thought she heard. Janine told him those were her favorite painters. I'm pretty sure she's never seen a single one of their paintings."

"Thank you," Ruth said to the waitress. "That's very helpful indeed."

We ate the Boston Cream Pie and gave the waitress a typical tip. We didn't want her to take note of us. Luckily I didn't have the sort of blue eyes women fell into so Janine didn't come over to say hello.

We finished and went outside into the sun.

Ruth put her arms around me and gave me a big kiss.

"Oh, Mr. Ryder. I'm now officially a fixer."

"And a great one," I said.

I don't think she could have made a wider smile.

We moved along the sidewalks, stopped for the lights, looked into shop windows, bought some ice cream.

We almost felt normal.

"So what do we do next, Mr. Ryder? You've got to let me help you now. Should I get a gun?"

I stared at her. "No weapons yet."

Then I told her what we were going to do next.

CHAPTER TWELVE

I walked by a store with a War Bonds poster in the window. The bonds were really needed. We would win the war in Europe and then in Japan, but we needed the money. I liked seeing the poster. I had bought a lot of War Bonds and used to sell them to people who might not otherwise be considered patriotic.

There were two men following me. They weren't hoods. Their suits looked like a uniform. I like to think I would have figured it out anyway, but I recognized one of the men who had followed me twice before.

I therefore wasn't surprised when a limousine car door opened. The driver, moving faster than I could, opened the back door. The two men following me got closer. One of my followers trotted a few steps and put his hand on my left shoulder. He didn't squeeze hard, just hard enough to tell me not to run because I wasn't going to be going anywhere.

The speedy driver looked at me, and said, "Someone would like to speak with you."

They didn't toss me into the back seat or stick a weapon in the small of my back or threaten the continuing health of my heart.

I nodded at the driver and climbed in.

"You knew it would be me, didn't you?" The voice came from the man sitting beside me.

"Yes," I said. "You shouldn't use the same people to follow me. Have some respect please."

He bowed his head.

The man I continued to call Agent Madison, although I knew his real name, had recruited me for an undercover FBI operation and then another one.

He had grown a bit grayer, but on him it looked distinguished. His skin was tight across his face.

"How have you been, Ryder?"

"It's so nice that the federal government cares about my well-being." I paused. "I have stuff to do. Why am I here?"

"You met a woman named Sister Grace."

"I have a wide circle of acquaintances."

"That may be, but not all of them are raising money and putting themselves and others in danger in Europe or smuggling children illegally into the United States."

"What? You're afraid those children will grow up to be bank robbers?"

He ignored me.

"Did Sister Grace hire you, Ryder?"

"She didn't give me a penny."

"Maybe not, but you have this utterly strange habit of helping people and not charging them. Did you reach an agreement with her?"

"I agreed to look into a murder in New York. A friend of hers had a daughter who was killed. There are no illegalities involved. And not a single dangerous child."

"Don't let the habit fool you. She has steel inside. She'll stop at nothing. She wants to save those children and doesn't care who she puts in danger. She doesn't care about American laws. She won't let anything stand in her way."

"That's pretty understandable, isn't it Agent Madison?"

"From her point of view, sure. I've seen more reports about the Jews in Europe than you have Ryder. It's much, much worse than anybody is saying in public. One doctor, a doctor mind you, lines kids up to see how many heads a single bullet can go through. And I've seen photographs that would give a Marine nightmares. So don't tell me about it. But we have a State Department. We have regulations."

"If you've seen those photographs, maybe you should leave Sister Grace and her friends to their business and get on with protecting America."

"Look, Ryder. You've helped us. A lot. We're grateful. No one wants to see you get in so deep you can't dig yourself out. Sister Grace will get some money and go back to Europe. You might consider staying away from her until then."

"I'm going to try to solve a murder. That's all I've got to do with her group. For now."

"And what does that mean, Ryder?"

I stared at him.

"Roosevelt knows what is going on in Europe with the Jews. He doesn't help them."

"He has a war to fight."

"He might try saving some lives along the way. We owe the people there all we can give. We're talking about children. I'm going to help if I can."

"You won't be able to help very much from a jail cell."

"You'll have to catch me first."

"We're the FBI. We're pretty good at that."

"You can start by getting different people to follow me."

"Tell me about the murder."

I told Madison the whole story. Normally I wouldn't do that, but I wondered if he had or could get information that I couldn't.

He was silent as I talked.

When I finished, he said, "The jeweler is going to give Sister Grace a lot of money, right? And Sister Grace is going to use it to bring children over here and bribe people to let them in?"

I was silent.

"I'm not as stupid as you thought, huh, Ryder?"

"I would think you would be concentrating on getting Nazi sympathizers and spies and murderers off the street."

"I want to talk to you off the record."

"You can't do that here." All our words were being recorded.

"There's a diner around the corner, Ryder. Let's walk to it. The other customers have been cleared out.

"Sure. I'm hungry."

We walked over. As Madison had said, we were the only ones in there besides the guy behind the counter.

I walked over to the last stool. I always sat there if I could because that stool offered the most counter space.

The guy behind the counter came over.

"What can I get you gentlemen?"

Madison said, "Just a cup of coffee."

I said, "A radio and a hot cup of coffee." The man nodded and left.

"A radio, Ryder? What are you talking about?'

"It's Hash House Greek, Agent Madison. The language spoken in greasy restaurants, the kind of place you walk in and slide to your seat."

"Okay. Educate me. What exactly does it mean to order a radio in here?"

I shrugged. "To down a piece of bread is to toast it."

"Okay. I get that."

"I ordered tuna on toast."

"I'm not hearing radio yet."

"So tuna on toast becomes tuna down. You hear tuna down enough it begins to sound like tune 'er down. A radio, Agent Madison."

"I'll stick to English."

"You'll miss the fun of language."

"I'll take my chances."

The man was gone. There was a good possibility he'd bring us back some food. Indeed, he brought the coffee over twenty seconds later.

When he again left, I said, "What don't you want the FBI to hear?"

"There's a warehouse in Queens, by the airport. Sort of pleasant place inside. Right now it's got some prisoners. Children prisoners. Illegal children prisoners."

"You sending them up the river?"

"They're going back to Europe in a week."

I raised my voice. "Are you crazy? You're handing children over to the Nazis to be killed."

"Orders from the State Department. I just follow orders. I don't question them."

He took a sip of coffee.

Then he continued. "This Thursday night between six and eight the warehouse is amazingly not going to be guarded. Someone with a few trucks could make quite a haul."

"I'm curious. What's the address of this warehouse?"

He reached into his pocket and took out a card. It had the address on it.

I looked at the card, raised my face and stared at Agent Madison. "Mr. Hoover might not approve."

"You'd be surprised at what Mr. Hoover approves. I told you. We've seen photographs that will never be released to the public."

"He know about this operation?"

"Of course not. And don't get caught. There are plenty of people that would love to catch the Jews trying to sneak into this country, children or not. Don't let that happen."

My food came and I ate it slowly. Madison just sat there and read a paper that someone had left.

When I finished eating, I said, "It's nice that there's a human being somewhere inside you."

"I do my best to keep it hidden."

"Those children deserve a chance."

"You don't have to tell me, Ryder. People are convinced I used to be a child myself. I personally don't believe it."

He hesitated. He had more to tell me. More FBI classified information.

Telling me won out over remaining silent.

"The Nazis are going after the nun."

"I know," I said.

"You know about Tristan?"

I shook my head. "Just the name. And that he wants to kill Sister Grace."

"And people who help her, Ryder. You put a big fat target on yourself."

I pursed my lips.

"What can you tell me about Tristan?"

"We don't know a lot. Gestapo-trained. A reputation as someone without regrets or feelings. Serving Hitler is his whole purpose."

"Any idea of his real name?"

"No."

"Any idea what he looks like?"

"I'd guess the Aryan ideal. But that's not based on knowledge."

"Are you looking for him?"

"We're looking for every Nazi agent. Of course we're looking for him. But his whole training is how to be invisible. He'll have money, weapons, a list of people to go to for help. He'll have special training. This isn't some gangster, Ryder. This is a professional killer."

"Specialties?"

"Yeah. Murder without caring. I'm just telling you to watch out. And I mean in a serious way. You're good. You spot my people following you. But one man you don't know. That's a different problem. My men are trained. But they're human. They haven't had their consciences surgically removed. Tristan will stop at nothing. Whatever causes you to take your time, slow down, and take care. Normal morality has no effect on him at all. You have to get even smarter. Get even tougher."

We sat in silence for a few seconds and then got up and walked outside into the blazing sunlight which even burned through the city's soot.

CHAPTER THIRTEEN

I made it over to West 53rd a little before eleven. The streets were more crowded than I expected for such a cold day.

I know the names of maybe ten painters. I'm ashamed of this. One of the customers in the diner said the word "ignorant" came from the word "ignore" and if in fact I was ignorant about painters that was because I had ignored them. He was right about that. There were gaps the size of the Grand Canyon in my knowledge. The older I got the less able I was to shove them aside.

I walked up to the desk.

"Hi, my name is Jack Ryder. I'm looking for a guy named Peter. He is arranging an exhibition that begins here next month. Something about realists."

The young woman looked shocked that someone without adequate taste had made his way into MoMA.

"The exhibit, sir, is 'Americans 1943: Realists and Magic Realists.' It will be held from February 10th to March 21st. Please come and learn about your history."

I gave my best smile, which, with kindness, might simply be called pathetic.

"Thank you. And Peter."

"Peter Jensen is working hard on the exhibit, sir." She handed me some kind of map.

"He is here, in this office." She had marked it off. I felt like a lost little boy wandering around in an adult world.

I made my way to the office.

A good-looking man was sitting at the desk. His pale face was trapped between utter anguish and awe.

"Mr. Jensen?"

He looked up.

"Unless you're here to give me an extra two days in my life, I don't have time to speak with you."

"It's about Rebecca Lonigan."

He stared at me. His face was unusually expressive. He now looked wounded and full of sadness.

"What's your name and are you with the police?"

"I'm Jack Ryder and I'm helping the police," I said. I left my role vague. People can fill in the details the way that they want.

"I really don't have much time, but tell me if you have found Rebecca's killers."

"I'm sorry to say we haven't."

"I'm working on Edward Hopper now for the exhibition. Do you know him?"

"I'm sorry. I don't."

He nodded. "His paintings are all about loneliness, how humans are separated from each other. The darkness we all live in. I think of Rebecca when I look at Hopper's paintings." He paused for a few seconds.

"Mr. Ryder, how may I help the police?"

"Her father did not know about you?"

"No. But I don't see how my relationship with Rebecca helps solve her murder."

"Ah, Mr. Jensen, you walked around with her. You sat at restaurants or went to the movies. Maybe you came across her friends. Maybe it was one of those friends who killed her."

He shook his head vigorously.

"You simply don't understand Rebecca. She and I broke up and I still had deep feelings for her and she me. It was just that her family or maybe it was the world would not let us be together. I met some of her friends. But not many because she was trying to keep the relationship away from her father specifically and generally very private, even hidden."

Peter looked out the window for a few seconds and then turned back to face me.

"Everyone we met who knew her loved her. She was a wonderful person. Mr. Ryder, as I understand it, she was in that bakery at the wrong time. I can't think that the killers were after her."

"Do you know much about the father's jewelry business?"

"I met her there a couple of times when he was out of town. But, no, I didn't know much about the business at all. Why do you ask?"

"The father's wealth opens up a lot of possibilities. A business rival. Someone who fairly or unfairly felt cheated. Maybe the father took out a loan from someone and was late paying the loan back."

His mouth opened a little.

"I would hate to inhabit your mind, Mr. Ryder. It is filled with darkness and disgust. Hopper is dark enough for me. And he hangs on the wall. I don't know anyone in the world you ask about."

It was time.

"Exactly where were you when the bakery robbery took place, Mr. Jensen?"

"Please leave, sir. People will insult me because of my catalog or my choice for the exhibit. I accept that. I do not accept being accused of murder."

"I'll leave Mr. Jensen. Just as soon as you tell me where you were. I seriously hope it is not necessary to bring you down to police headquarters or subject you to a line-up with other suspects."

"You are a disgusting man."

"Perhaps. But if so I'm a disgusting man still waiting for an answer."

"I remember perfectly. I was doing research at the New York Public Library." Jensen's voice was filled with disgust.

"And before you ask me, Mr. Ryder, there were loads of witnesses but no one who knew me by name."

"Did you request any books?"

His face brightened. "Yes. I did. And I had to fill out a form. My name will be on it. You can check with them. Now, will you please leave?"

I half-bowed and walked out of the Museum. I went for a cup of coffee and a piece of apple pie.

I thought as I drank the coffee. It was true that Rebecca Lonigan sounded too good. Maybe the real girl was imprisoned inside her and never had a chance to get out. That happened to a lot of bright women.

But it was also possible that I was being stubborn. How many times did I have to hear that no one wanted to kill her? From what I had learned about her father, he was honest. There were no loans I could find. I was sure he dealt with some people with less than savory reputations, but his business wasn't failing. That meant everyone was doing well. There was no reason to go after him or his family.

I so wanted to solve the case for Sister Grace and the Lonigans, father and daughter, that I was too focused. Maybe it was just a robbery. Maybe Della Benson, the other woman in the store, was the real target.

I was overwhelmed at that moment by my sense of being a failure. I allowed my emotions to bathe me for a moment. Then I straightened up and walked outside into the cold.

I wasn't about to quit. I wasn't about to let those children in Europe down.

I tightened my lips and went on.

CHAPTER FOURTEEN

Vinny called. The trucks and drivers were ready. I called the Hotel Fourteen and spoke to Sister Grace. I said I couldn't tell her any of the details for her own protection, but I needed to know where to bring the children.

She hesitated. She knew this could be a trap. If I had gone to the FBI, they may have used fake children for bait. But, I reasoned, if she thought it might be a trap, wouldn't I want her to be along for the so-called rescue? She took a chance and told me the location of a house where I could bring the children.

It was a building in Manhattan. That was good. It meant the children wouldn't be in the trucks for a long time.

And Vinny had decided it might look suspicious to have several civilian trucks in a sort of convoy. The cops might pull us over.

So, against my own judgment, I agreed the trucks could be separated. I would be nervous until they all arrived. One flat tire and they'd probably need to get a doctor for me.

It was late Thursday afternoon when I made another decision. I called Detective Simon Hill and told him what I was doing that night. I asked him for help. I didn't really need his help, but I thought it would matter to him if he saved some children.

"Flash for you, Ryder. I need a calculator to figure out how many laws you're breaking."

"Those are only human laws, Detective. I'm obeying the bigger laws."

"You're going to land me in human jail one day, Ryder."

"You don't have to go, Detective. I felt I had to ask. I thought it would be good for you."

"Oh, I'm going. You couldn't keep me away."

We all met on the street outside the diner. Gertie had packed food for everyone, including the children.

Hill rode next to the driver of one car. I was in a second truck. The drivers gathered together and we went over the different routes we would take. One guy had checked the weather and the traffic. I calculated there would only be a ten minute difference between the arrival of the first truck at our destination and the arrival of the final truck.

We guessed the time for us all to drive to the Queens warehouse, and I gave the signal to begin. Sitting there in the truck, I suddenly had a flash of the real dangers Sister Grace and her supporters faced driving in Nazi Europe not in Manhattan and Queens. Again, I was furious with my failed heart that had not allowed me to be in the Army.

The night had a bit of fog, so the truck I was in moved slowly. Of course, there was an accident between two cars along the way and that further slowed us down.

The rescue of the children would not begin until I arrived, so the delays were infuriating.

Finally, we got to the parking area. Two other trucks were already there. That was a good sign. One more to go. It arrived no more than five minutes later. I realized I was glad I was late. It saved me from the intense worry I would have felt if I got to the warehouse and had to wait for the other trucks.

Detective Hill came over to me.

"You're sure there are no guards in there? I'm not shooting anybody."

"That's what I was promised." I didn't tell him that it was the FBI that promised me. The men from Vinny had come early in their own cars because we needed the truck space for the children. I wouldn't want to take on these guys. They were Vinny's toughest, and that meant they were the city's toughest.

They all followed behind me. I went to the warehouse's front door.

I was surprised because it was quiet inside. I snapped open the lock, opened the door, and walked inside.

The children were seated on the ground. They looked at me and the men behind me in horror. I hadn't thought of that. I didn't want them to scream. But instead of wild yelling, they stared at us in stunned silence.

I walked over and began handing out candy bars. Maybe a dentist wouldn't approve, but the children did. There was a sudden bond between us.

They took the candy but didn't eat it. They didn't even unwrap the bars.

I suddenly understood they were afraid of being poisoned. So I took a bar and ate it.

Suddenly there was a satisfying sound of candy bar wrappers being torn.

I walked over to the front row of the children.

"Does anybody speak English?"

Another problem I had not even considered. The Army was probably better off without me.

One of Vinny's men tapped me on the shoulder.

"Mr. Ryder?"

I turned.

"Yes."

"My name is Berger. Vinny thought it would be a good idea if there was someone along who could speak Yiddish. I'm the guy."

I couldn't speak, so I just nodded.

Berger stood in front of me. Whatever he said, the children laughed. It was the most wonderful sound in the world.

Berger talked to them. I suppose he was telling them about what was going to happen.

They didn't move.

Berger turned to me.

"They're scared. They think we're going to take them to a camp."

"My God. Tell them Sister Grace is waiting for them. Tell them anything, Berger. Anything. But get them on the trucks."

Berger talked to them.

I checked my watch. Our narrow window of time would shut if we didn't start moving.

Berger turned back to me.

"They don't believe me. One little boy said the men all look scary."

Detective Hill had been listening.

"What do we do, Ryder?"

I turned to Berger.

"Any ideas?"

"Can we get this Sister Grace here? I think it would take her telling them to go for them to get up and follow us."

"We don't have the time," I said.

One little girl got up. Her face was streaked with dirt. Her dark hair and dark eyes were filled with horror.

She went up to Berger and began talking to him.

He came over to me.

"That little girl said she believed you, Ryder. She said you had a truthful face."

"And so?"

"So, Ryder, she said the children won't leave voluntarily. That we should pick them up and take them."

I stared at Hill.

"What's our choice?" Hill asked.

I looked at him.

"I learned about twenty words of Hebrew from various people. One person told me in the Land of Israel they said of an impossible choice like we have, 'Ein Breira,' there is no alternative."

I stared at Hill.

"There is no alternative, Detective. We have to carry them to the trucks."

"But they'll scream and kick."

"I know. Ein Breira."

I signaled to Vinny's men.

Berger told the little girl what we were going to do.

She stood there, maybe eight years old, and she spoke in a clear voice to the children.

Berger translated as she spoke. She told them we were taking them to a safe place. That the warehouse was the danger, not us. She said they would get food. I hadn't thought of that.

There was still resistance as Vinny's men picked the children up and took them to the trucks. But their resistance mostly consisted of crying and kicking.

I checked my watch and told the men to hurry.

We had twenty minutes before the warehouse guards returned.

We got the children on the truck. I was shocked. Vinny's men were careful. They smiled. The toughest thugs in New York were smiling.

I waited until all the other trucks had left. Then I got in mine and pulled out.

I checked my watch.

We had plenty of time to go before the guards returned.

If two minutes was plenty of time.

CHAPTER FIFTEEN

I was in the diner again the afternoon after the rescue. The children had been very quiet in the trucks. They were scared and were busy resigning themselves to some horrible fate.

Sister Grace met us and helped reassure the children.

I sat and re-played what had happened. I realized that for the first time in a long while I felt good about myself.

Tommy called. I had asked him to check to see if there had been any additional information drawn from the corpses of the two victims.

We said hello and Tommy got right to it.

"Two nice ladies from what I hear, Ryder. Neither was pregnant. If there was a motive they didn't hear about it in the morgue. Everyone says a stupid robbery gone wrong. I know that doesn't help any, but I didn't want to mislead you."

I saw Detective Hill walking into the diner, so I wanted to wrap it up with Tommy.

"Keep listening," I said.

"You do know I mostly deal with dead people."

"They're great. They don't talk back."

"Ah, sometimes they do. I can hear in your voice that you want to get rid of me, Ryder. Story of my life. But I understand. I'll keep looking."

"Thanks, Tommy."

Hill sat down opposite me.

Ruth rushed over when she saw him sitting down.

"Ah," he said, "My favorite waitress."

"Hey," Gertie called out from behind the counter.

Hill laughed. "Sorry, Gertie, but Ruth gives me extra big slices of pie."

"She'd be in trouble if her uncle didn't own the place," Gertie yelled back.

Hill looked up at Ruth.

"I can't tell you how good you look to me," Hill said to her.

"Why, Detective, I do believe you're flirting with a professional waitress."

"Is it working?"

"Oh, very well."

"Do you two know there's someone else here?"

They both laughed.

"Sorry, Ryder. But I mean it. Seeing Ruth's face, the dimples, the smile, all of it, is like medicine to me."

"Did you want to order, Detective Hill, or just go on praising me? If I had a preference I'd go with praise."

"I can do that, Ruth. But I'm hungry."

"The usual?"

"Yes ma'am."

"Coming right up, Detective."

She turned.

"I don't even have a usual," I said.

Hill shrugged.

"I like her."

"Great. It would be better if you waited until you weren't married any more before you like her."

"I know. I can't help my feelings, though."

"Of course you can help your feelings."

Hill wanted to change the conversation.

"Thanks for taking me along last night. It was great to do something useful. All day I deal with the scum of the earth. Last night I felt clean."

"It was good."

Ruth came back and talked again with Detective Hill.

I just ate in silence.

I was thinking about what I had to do next.

CHAPTER SIXTEEN

It is easy to mislead yourself when you investigate. Here I had a victim to focus on. Rebecca Lonigan was so laudable a person, so sympathetic, so kind. And so dead.

I had an extraordinary cause that pushed my focus on her beyond her character. I had a righteous cause.

And I forgot the first rules of the fixer.

Look at the evidence. See the truth, not what you want to see. Be ready to change based on logic and evidence.

I had looked at Rebecca Lonigan. And looked again. And again. I couldn't come up with any reason why someone would want to kill her. So, the bakery robbery and murders were either a random incident or just maybe one of the other two people there was the target.

It didn't make sense that the wounded owner was the target. If you wanted a store owner you went in when he was alone. And you made sure he was dead. Maybe the arm wouldn't be your perfect target.

And so there I was. Either it was all random or it was Mrs. Della Benson.

I pulled my eyes and mind away from Rebecca and looked at the other murder victim.

I called Benson's sister and arranged to interview her. She claimed over the phone not to possess any information about the robbery. In that she was correct.

But I knew all about the robbery. I didn't know enough about Della.

Della's sister lived in a small apartment on the Lower East Side. She lived alone. There was a picture on a table in the living room. The picture was of a man in uniform.

The apartment was clean and ordered. The furniture was covered so it wouldn't get dirty.

Olive Randall was in that in-between age. Her good looks were still there but in retreat. Age was boldly exerting itself and beauty had decreasing chances to stand out.

She offered me a cup of coffee. I thanked her. We sat at the kitchen table. She had been crying, anticipating having to go over the details once again. I admired her red-faced determination. She could have just told me she had been through it all with the police and needed silence about her sister.

"This is good coffee," I said to her.

"Yes," she said. "I can put that on my tombstone. 'She Made Good Coffee.' There's not much else that is worth it to put there."

"You're a commercial artist, aren't you?"

She nodded. "I help sell products. I call it artistry so I can sleep at night. Really I sell people what they don't need at prices they often can't afford."

She paused for a few seconds to stare at me.

"You have a dreadful occupation yourself, Mr. Ryder."

"Do I? How so?"

"You deal with death and low human motives. You trample on the privacy of people and families. And, no offense, but I bet that sometimes you create a bigger mess than you clean up. Maybe you accuse the wrong person. Maybe, Mr. Ryder, you get an innocent person killed."

"There's good to do in the world, Miss Randall. I do my best. But you're right. Sometimes it's not good enough."

She made a facial gesture at me. It was somewhere between a smile and a smirk.

"Did you just have morbid curiosity about me, Mr. Ryder? Did you just want to meet the poor victim's sister so you could stare up-close at grief?"

"Miss Randall, I came to get information. At any moment that I'm disturbing you, I will leave. My goal is to find your sister's killer. It would be a fool's errand to promise that I will succeed. All I can do is promise not to give up before moral and physical exhaustion sets in."

"What do you want, Mr. Ryder?"

"Tell me about your sister," I said.

"Della seemed to have had a bright future. She was a good-looking girl. Every boy we knew thought so. My father wanted her to go to college. That was unusual for men. Usually they wanted their daughters to stay unmarried in the house to take care of their aging parents. But our father was different. He worked his whole life. He was born in Pennsylvania and as a child he knew what it was like to go into a mine all day. He hated it. Later he moved to New York and opened a toy store. It was heaven for Della and me. He didn't want his two daughters to work like he had.

"But Della didn't listen. She sees a handsome guy and she's gotta get married. It's a mistake women make. They confuse looks with character."

"Men make the same mistake," I said.

She nodded. "That they do. But they're men. They can get away with it. Anyway, Della met this guy. Worked in a bowling alley. Now there's a future. Anyway she thinks they made a cute couple. Which is a wonderful reason to get married.”

I had to be careful with the next part.

“I take it the marriage wasn’t perfect.”

Olive Randall gave out a harsh laugh.

“You might say that. You also might say that her handsome husband was systematically working his way through the Manhattan phone book in search of women.”

“How did he end up in the Army?”

“Adventure. You want my opinion, he liked the idea of searching out foreign women. He figured he’d come across widows and single women.”

“That’s a strange reason to join the Army.”

“Maybe I’m wrong. Maybe he got caught up in the patriotism after the attack on Pearl Harbor. Anyway, he joined. And he fought. I’ll give him that. At least he fought until he got himself shot.”

“I understand he was in a hospital when your sister was attacked.”

“She was killed. She wasn’t attacked. Don’t try to be delicate. It doesn’t suit a man like you.”

“Sorry.”

“All right. I hired a detective to double-check. I thought maybe he was the one who shot her.”

“A lot of couples fight and it doesn’t lead to a shooting.”

“If you knew him you’d have double-checked as well. But he was in some kind of hospital. It saved him the cost of a divorce.”

“Had your sister seen a lawyer?”

“Of course. You live and pay attention, you grow up. She recognized what he was, and she recognized what she had become. She wanted out.”

"I need to ask you an indelicate question, Miss Benson."

"More indelicate than murder?"

"Maybe."

"All right. Go ahead and ask. You seem smarter than everyone else I've met working on my sister's death."

"I'm good at fooling people."

"But not yourself, I bet. Ask your indelicate question."

"Was he violent?"

"Why do you ask? He wasn't in the States."

"Simple curiosity."

"Which translates into you don't want to tell me. All right. Yes. He was violent. You're really asking me if he hit her."

"I wouldn't want to try to get something by you."

"No, you wouldn't. This is between us, Mr. Ryder. He hit her. It's the story of a million marriages. He drank. He eyed other women. He was frustrated by how life treated him. He'd come home. She'd say something and it would set him off. So he'd slug her."

"Ever send her to the hospital?"

"A couple of times. But you know what happened. She said she fell. It wasn't like every week. Maybe twice a year. But finally the hitting and all the other stuff added up and she decided to get a divorce. She couldn't afford it, but she didn't care."

"Do you know anything about his life in the Infantry?"

"You should talk to his best friend. Kenny talked about him all the time."

"Do you know the friend's name?"

"Yeah. It is Markie Fuller. I don't know what the 'Markie' is short for. I do know that he came back to the States. I'm not sure why. But Markie could tell you Army stories. Although, again, Mr. Ryder, you'll excuse me but it sounds as though you're just wasting your time."

"Information is never a waste of time."

Olive Randall shook her head.

"It is if it robs you of the moments you need to stay on what matters. Kenny Benson wasn't here. He couldn't have shot my sister. There's no reason to learn any more about him."

"Maybe you're right. Maybe that's just how I work. So do you have any idea of Markie Fuller's address or phone number?"

"Nope."

We talked for twenty more minutes. She was lonely and wanted to keep talking to me. I liked talking to her.

Finally, we said good-bye.

I started walking along the cold streets. The wind seemed to go right through me, and I shivered.

I never heard it.

All of a sudden, a car whizzed by in the street next to me. A hand reached out.

A shot sounded.

I didn't have time to duck or even move.

The car was driving off by the time I reacted.

A man on the sidewalk ran up to me.

"Are you all right, mister?"

"Thanks. I'm fine," I said.

"You're lucky his aim was off."

I nodded.

But the man was wrong. The shooter had perfect

aim. He meant just to warn me. He hit some brick behind me, just missing a store window.

"Do you want me to call the cops?"

I shook my head.

"They have enough trouble tracking killers. No one was hurt here."

"I guess you're right. I'd be scared out of my mind."

"If I had any sense, I would be too," I said.

But I was too busy thinking to be scared. I knew I was going to break-in to a house that night and I was considering the best way to do it.

CHAPTER SEVENTEEN

"Why aren't you eating, Mr. Ryder?"

I looked up at Ruth. Her face was full of concern. I liked that.

"I have a job to do tonight. I'm waiting for it to get a bit later. The clouds are rolling in. That's good for me."

"What kind of a job, Mr. Ryder?"

I stared at her.

"I'm not sure I should tell you, Ruth."

"Hmm. So it's illegal. And it's late and dark. And you want more of a cloud cover." She paused. "Where are you breaking into, Mr. Ryder?"

"I've created a female Jesse James."

"Please Mr. Ryder. He robbed good people. And he got shot. I'm trying to help you do good and stay alive."

"I'm breaking into an apartment, Ruth."

Her mouth opened.

"Will there be people in the apartment when you break in?"

"There aren't supposed to be."

"Why aren't they there?"

"Della Benson was the woman who lived there."

"One of the women killed in the bakery."

"Right."

"But doesn't she have a husband?"

"Right now Mr. Benson is in a hospital some-place overseas thanks to the United States Army. There shouldn't be anybody in the apartment."

"But what if there is? What if, say, Mr. Benson's cousin needed a place to stay?"

"That's the burglar's dilemma. You can't account for all the possible problems. Finally you do your best to figure it out and just gamble."

"Oh. Say, Mr. Ryder, do they have a lot of gold and diamonds in the apartment? No, never mind. You're not a thief. So what do they have?"

"I hope they have an address of someone I'm looking for."

"And that's all you want, Mr. Ryder? What kind of break-in is that?"

I smiled at her.

"You can't go, Ruth. It's not the kind of training I want to give you."

"But it's exactly the kind of training I need. We're not really stealing. There won't be anyone there. It's sort of a safe burglary. Perfect for training a new fixer."

Another pause.

"Please."

"I suppose I could use a look-out."

"I'd be perfect for that, Mr. Ryder. But two people looking for an address is better than one person. Isn't that right? Or whatever you need. Oh, I think this would be a big step forward in my training."

"I think I should ask Gertie."

"Oh, don't do that Mr. Ryder. She's too protective. She'd have me stay in my apartment all the time."

"She knows the world all too well, Ruth."

"So, can I go?"

"Against my judgment and conscience, you can."

We waited an hour. Ruth told Gertie that she had a stomach ache and had to go home. There never were many customers at that time of night. Gertie would have agreed even if Ruth's uncle didn't own the diner. I said I would see her home. Gertie nodded. She knew she didn't have to worry about me taking advantage of Ruth.

I had already plotted the shortest distance and the best route from the diner to the Benson apartment building. I had also checked. I figured it wasn't fancy enough to have a doorman, but I had checked earlier in the day. No doorman.

It was dark when we got there. It was easy to get into the lobby. The front door wasn't locked. The tenants weren't paying extra for security, and that meant they weren't going to get it.

"What's the apartment number, Mr. Ryder?" Ruth was whispering.

"203," I whispered back. We found the stairs and walked up a flight.

I started to go into the corridor, but Ruth stopped me.

"I'll look, Mr. Ryder. I look less suspicious than you do."

I nodded.

She checked and signaled me to follow her. We had gotten into the corridor, found the apartment, and were standing in front of it when we heard the elevator door open.

Ruth grabbed me and started kissing me. She very effectively blocked our faces. Whoever was in the elevator got out and turned away from us. We heard him unlock his door. Then he opened it again. He must have thought we were very passionate since we were still kissing. He stared at us, decided we weren't Bonnie and Clyde, and went back inside.

"You're some kisser, Ruth."

"I'm a bit out of practice, Mr. Ryder."

"It doesn't show."

She smiled.

We found the door. I tried various keys I had, but again the tenants weren't paying enough and so the third key worked.

We walked inside.

I put on the lights.

"Close the curtains, please Ruth."

She nodded and went to perform the task.

I went around the apartment.

One bedroom. Cheap furniture. Dusty. A desk was in what I suspect counted as the living room. I'd get to that. I went into the kitchen.

Normal people hide their valuables in very predictable places. Why they think, for example, that no one was going to look in the freezer is unclear to me. Some people do better. They have a safe in the front hallway, cover it up with a nice material and maybe even put a vase filled with colorful flowers on it. Thieves, they think, will walk right past it and miss the safe. Or, if they want to take the trouble, they unscrew the light plate and tie something valuable by a piece of string and then put the plate back where it belonged. Or in a lot of other standard places. Or they've read Poe and leave it in plain sight.

None of it works against a trained thief.

Ruth came over to me.

"Where do I start, Mr. Ryder?"

"You know kitchens better than I do."

"And it's not fair. That's where they send girls."

"We're not dealing with fair. We're dealing with

finding the address."

"You told me the guy's name is Markie Fuller. Do you know what city he lives in?"

"No. My guess is it's not New York, though."

Ruth went off to look.

I would look in the desk last.

I went to the bedroom. If the address were really important, Kenny Benson would always have it close to home when he was here. So, if say he had to get up quickly in the middle of the night he wouldn't want to have to scramble for it but have it immediately available.

Of course, since he was far away from home, he could have carried it on him. Maybe he was sitting up in his hospital bed at that very second starting at it.

I couldn't find the address near the bed. I lifted the corners of the mattress, got down and put a flashlight under the bed, touched the blanket all over for a tell-tale sign of a hidden object, felt inside the pillow cases, went through the bureau near the bed, and looked in the clothes closet. I sent Ruth to go through the shoes in the bottom of the closet.

"I have a feeling you're giving me all the dirty jobs to discourage me, Mr. Ryder."

"You have to see that a fixer is not a job for those who search for glamour."

Then I went to the desk. It was an obvious place, which made me think an address wouldn't be there. But then not again Kenny Benson was not exactly a criminal mastermind.

I found a bunch of letters in their envelopes in the second drawer on the right.

I flipped through the envelopes.

And there it was.

Marquis Fuller
Cherry Hill Road
Sag Harbor, New York

I got up and tapped Ruth on the shoulder.

She turned around.

"I was shocked, Mr. Ryder. There were no coded messages in the shoes."

"You've still done a good job, Ruth."

"You found the address."

"I did. Now let's get out of here."

It was just then that we heard the front door open.

CHAPTER EIGHTEEN

Ruth grabbed my arm. I took her hand and led her to the window by the fire escape.

"Did you see them come in here?" The voice was sharp, filled with a lifetime of cigar smoke.

"I saw them kissing right in front of this door. I knew right away they didn't belong. The guy who lives here is a soldier."

"Yeah. Okay. So you called me. So I'll look around."

"You manage the place, Sal. It's your job."

"And I'm doing it."

We were a room away from them. I started to open the window. And, I suppose if it had moved, we might have gone out of the window. As it was, it didn't move and we were stuck in the apartment. With the lights on.

I suppose I could have taken a chair and broken the window, but we would never have gotten out in time.

It was time for an alternate plan. I would have felt better if I had one.

"Come on," I said to Ruth.

"We're going out there? To see those men?"

"We are."

We stepped into the living room and came face to face with the two men.

"Who are you?" I said. "And what are you doing in my cousin's apartment?"

One guy stepped forward. "I'm Sal. I manage the building. You don't rent this apartment."

"That's true. But my cousin, Kenny Benson, does.

He's in a hospital overseas right now and he asked me to send him some information."

I held up the piece of paper with Markie Fuller's address.

"He never said anything to me."

I took a step forward.

"Listen, sir. Kenny's wife was killed in a bakery shooting not long ago. He doesn't have time to deal with little details. He needed this for some reason and he asked me to get it."

I decided to back off a bit.

"All right. I'm sorry. You're right. Maybe my wife here and I should have asked your permission, but it's late, we're tired, and I just wanted to get it done."

"Well, this gentleman here saw you kissing in the hall and thought you looked suspicious."

"Men still kiss their wives. Some men and some wives anyway."

"How come you ain't in the Army?"

I tapped my chest.

"Bad ticker. I'd love to shoot some Nazis." It was the first honest answer I'd given.

The man who had seen us spoke up. "I don't like it. I think you should call the cops."

"Shut up," Sal the manager said. "Cops do not like to be disturbed. They don't like it when people report what might or might not be a crime. They drive out here and what? Call Europe to check if this guy is really a cousin?"

Sal turned to me.

"I'm goin' to walk around. I see anything valuable gone, I am gonna call the cops."

"The radio is there. There's nothing disturbed.

Kenny doesn't exactly keep loads of cash in here. He doesn't have loads of cash to keep."

I pointed to Ruth. "Besides, does she look like a thief?"

"No," Sal said, "but you do."

"I can take care of myself."

That was meant as a message to the two gentlemen.

Sal looked around. He couldn't find anything missing so he came back and stood in front of us.

"Search him," the guy who saw us kissing said.

"No. I ain't gonna search him. It looks like everything is all right. But him and the missus are gonna leave like right now."

I held up my hands.

"Hey, we're outta here. I got what Kenny wanted. If I didn't we'd have an argument. But I did."

I took Ruth's hand. We slowly walked toward the front door. I could feel Ruth shaking.

We walked outside and were both silent as we went through the dark and dangerous streets.

We made it back to the diner. Neither of us had said a word.

We went inside.

"You two look awful," Gertie said. "Sit down and I'll get you some coffee."

"Yeah," Ruth said, "with scotch in it."

Ruth didn't drink, so Gertie laughed. When she went to get the coffee, Ruth said to me. "I think I'm going to be sick."

"No you're not. You're a tough fixer."

"I'm a weak waitress. Maybe I should stick to newspapers for now."

"You did great."

"I can't move."

We sat for an hour. At some point Ruth began shaking and had some trouble stopping.

"How can you do that, Mr. Ryder? Come up with a story so fast?"

I shrugged. "It's part of the job."

"But you're not even shook up."

"I am inside. I'm just used to it."

Ruth turned to me.

"I don't want to be alone tonight."

"Maybe you should stay with Gertie or at your uncle's place."

She began crying.

"I'm sorry Ruth."

She just nodded. "You're not really sorry, Mr. Ryder or you would invite me back to your place. You called me your wife tonight."

"It was a little play, Ruth. You know that."

"Make it up to me then."

"And how do I do that Ruth?"

"Make me get right back in the saddle. Don't let me fall off the horse and stay crying on the ground. I've got to ride again and right away."

"And how do I do that?"

"Take me to Sag Harbor to look for Markie Fuller."

"You had a quick recovery, Ruth."

"Oh no I didn't. I'm still scared. I'm still shaking although now it's mostly inside. But I'm not a quitter, Mr. Ryder. I can't let fear stop me. Besides it's just a ride with you. We can talk some more. And we're just talking to a guy. No more breaking in or people questioning us. This is an easy way back. Please. If you won't take me back to your apartment, please do this."

"Go home and get some sleep. I'll call you in a few hours. I want to get started right away to Sag Harbor."

"I bet it's really cold out there. It's more open country. No buildings to keep the winds away."

"I'm not sure what the weather will be, Ruth."

"Oh, it will be cold. But we'll keep warm together, Mr. Ryder."

I looked at her.

She was delicate and easily hurt. She knew how I felt about my late wife. She knew I didn't date. She was needy and annoying. But she was also sweet and kind.

I nodded at her.

Then I went home to get a few hours of sleep.

Unless, like usual, I couldn't sleep.

CHAPTER NINETEEN

Ruth and I hit the road early. Riding into the wilds of Eastern Long Island was pleasant. The roads were narrow. The small towns were charming. The fresh air must have confused my lungs. The cows we passed decided we weren't a menace, and so they went back to munching grass.

We passed Water Mill. In Bridgehampton we stopped to get a sandwich. Ruth also ordered an ice cream soda. I took my coffee straight black.

There was a left turn to Sag Harbor. We went past a poor area and then were on Main Street. I wasn't sure where I was.

I parked, and we got out and walked. We passed "The Pierson Candy Shop and Restaurant" with their slogan: "A Good Store In A Good Town."

We saw the American Hotel on the right. We saw two older men on a bench. I asked them directions to Cherry Hill Road.

"Who ya looking for mister?" The man who asked had an interesting mix of teeth and empty spaces in his mouth.

"Markie Fuller."

The man nodded. "Good fellow, young Markie. Got shot in the war, you know. Don't mention it to him. He don't care to talk about it much."

"I won't. But first I have to get to him."

"What you got to see him for?"

"If I was looking to see you I wouldn't tell anybody your business."

The old man cackled.

"And you'd be right not to. We used to call that street Goats Alley 'cause of all the goats that went up and down it."

He gave me directions, which still seemed confusing, but he said everyone knows Markie and if I got confused I should just ask.

"What number is his house?"

The man laughed. "This here is Sag Harbor. It's nineteen and forty-three. We ain't got no numbers. We barely got phones. And even then we're mostly on party lines.

"Markie, he's got a big house in the middle of the block. Brown shingles and a red roof needs some repair, but Markie ain't quite able to get on that roof to fix it. You be good to him. The man's a national hero."

"Yes, sir. I will."

I was able to follow the directions pretty well. The house was indeed in need of repair, and not just the roof.

"We should have brought something," Ruth said. "Maybe food. Or a bottle of good scotch."

"I'm not exactly the Emily Post type."

"That's for sure."

We got out of the car and walked to the front door. I knocked.

A woman answered. She was thin with black, curly hair. She was probably only about thirty but life had tested her and she looked as though she kept failing the test.

"Good afternoon, ma'am," I said. "My name is Jack Ryder. This is my friend Ruth Draper. We'd like to see

Markie Fuller, if he's available."

The woman squinted.

"What you want to see Markie for?"

"To talk about Kenny Benson."

Her eyes widened, but she was good. She didn't move much.

"Kenny's fighting, protecting our country unlike some people who are standing on my porch trying to annoy my husband."

"I wish I could have fought, ma'am and I deeply admire your husband for doing so. I have a bad heart."

"And no courage."

"I assure you ma'am, I want to shoot Hitler more than you can imagine."

"How do you know Kenny?"

"I came here more to talk to your husband than to you, ma'am."

"You're kinda snippy, aren't you?"

"I've been called worse. Much worse."

"Come on. Markie don't get so many visitors. You be good to him. You and that painted lady you're with. You hear?"

"Yes, ma'am."

Markie was seated in a rocking chair. He couldn't have even reached his mid-thirties, but his hair was thinning, his eyes look as though someone had drained the life out of them, and his skin looked as though he had borrowed it from someone and didn't know how to wear it well.

I introduced myself and Ruth.

Fuller just nodded.

Then he said, "Where you from?"

"We drove out from New York just to see you."

He considered that for a few seconds.

"You're lucky you didn't get a ticket. Or did you?"

"No sir."

"It's the war, of course. We got a pleasure driving ban you see. Most people have adjusted and are using bus lines more and more. Unnecessary trips are no good. Was your trip necessary?"

"I'd like to think so. I wanted to speak with you about Kenny Benson."

"Yeah. We both got shot. Two good friends and we both got it. It was like the Nazis were looking for us."

"I'm sorry to hear about your injury."

"I'm fine. Every night I looked into the faces of my friends. Every night I knew I might not see them the next night. You know what that does to someone?"

"No, sir, I don't, but I imagine it's horrible."

"You're afraid to make friends. And I'll tell you what they don't say on the radio and don't show in the movies. Sometimes if we're running and those Nazis are shooting at us some men start laughing, right there as they watch others around them fall. I ain't smart enough to figure out why they laugh. Maybe they're just hysterical. Maybe they're glad they wasn't the ones that got shot. But it's a strange sight."

"Sir, we're kind of thirsty from the trip. Is it possible to get us a glass of water?"

"Yeah. It does get thirsty in the world." He called out to his wife and told her to get us some lemonade. She did so. We sat and drank it.

When we were half done, Fuller paused. "You know Kenny?"

"No, sir. I'm a private detective. I was hired by a man because his daughter was killed in a bakery hold-up.

Della Benson was the other victim in the robbery."

"Never met her. But I can tell you Kenny loved her. Some men they're a thousand miles from home. They're desperate in trouble. They could get killed any minute. They look for a friendly local girl. Maybe even a pro. But Kenny and me we weren't like that. No, sir. Kenny loved that woman."

Fuller took a sip from his blue mug.

"It near broke his heart."

"What did, if I may ask?"

"You really don't know?"

"No, sir."

"She wrote to him. I guess that thousand miles distance works both ways. She found herself another man. A man like you who got out of going to fight."

I was annoyed but tried not to show it.

"How did Kenny know that his wife had found another man?"

"She wrote him a Dear John letter. Said she was sorry. Said Kenny was a good man, but her heart had traveled down another road. Said she was going to see a lawyer. I don't know what hurt Kenny more, the bullets in him from the Nazis or that letter."

"Do you know the name of Mrs. Benson's new friend?"

"No. If he knew, Kenny never told me." He paused. "Faith." Fuller was calling to his wife. She came over to him.

"There's a letter Kenny wrote. We were supposed to write to some lawyer saying what a good man he was."

The man turned to me. "He was trying to stop any divorce."

Fuller's wife brought the letter over to him."

"Walter Anderson." He gave me an address on Park Avenue. That would have made Anderson one expensive lawyer.

"Thank you," I said.

"Don't know how that's gonna help you, but you should hear from someone more than me how good Kenny was. You say you was hired by the other victim's father?"

"That's right."

Fuller nodded.

"I suppose you're focusing on her, then. Why you asking about Kenny's wife?"

"Mr. Fuller, when you're a detective you have to learn everything about everybody. At least I do. It's like walking in the dark. You touch something and that sends you off in one direction."

"Leave Kenny be. He's suffered enough. He loved that woman. I wasn't there then but it broke his heart. He wrote me about it. Spent his night crying and wishing there had been some kind of mistake. Don't go poking around in his life. He's had it bad enough."

"I won't bother him at all, Mr. Fuller. I didn't even write him."

"Good. Leave it that way. When did you say you was leaving?"

"I said I was leaving right now."

"That sounds about right."

He adjusted himself in his rocker and began a steady rhythm going back and forth. It was a movement of dismissal.

Ruth and I thanked Mrs. Fuller and left.

I was quiet for most of the trip back. Ruth was smart enough to respect my need for the silence. I was thinking, sifting through what I had learned and placing it in the wider jigsaw puzzle of this case.

We got back to New York.

Gertie said I had messages from both Vinny and Tommy, and I said I'd call them the next morning.

Ruth stood there waiting for some kind of invitation from me. The situation couldn't go on like this. I hated the idea, but I thought I had to keep her away from my detective work and maybe away from me. It was cruel to keep seeming to encourage her. I thought I had been clear, but when it comes to desire, the heart hears what it wants to hear and disregards any contrary noise. It can look the facts straight in the face, nod at them in seeming understanding, and then just go on as if the stubborn facts weren't there. I admit I don't understand love, but I doubt anyone else does either.

CHAPTER TWENTY

I called Vinny first.

We traded gossip for a few minutes. This guy had found his way to prison. That guy fell out a window doing a burglary.

Then Vinny said, "You wanted some background on that guy Claude Martine. How much damage you want to do?"

"Nothing physical as I told you, Vinny. Punch him in his wallet. Hurt his business. That kind of stuff."

"All right. He owns a restaurant, so he's dirty. A lot of businesses are making money during the War. Some are doing it legitimate. The government is on a spending spree. But Martine he's making money just by buying his food in a special way."

"What are you talking about, Vinny?"

"He's dealing with Maxie Blake."

"The guy with the face like an ugly boxer dog?"

"That's the guy."

"What's Maxie doing for him?"

"Stopping meat trucks and gently telling the driver to hand over all he's got. Or get shot. For some reason, most of the drivers choose to hand over the meat."

"And Maxie sells the meat to Martine at a very reduced rate."

"Martine is making a fortune doing this because people know he's got the best food at a reasonable rate.

No one asks if the great steaks have been stolen."

I considered this.

"Maxie owe you any favors, Vinny?"

"One or two."

"You may have to call them in."

"You know, Ryder, you are a giant pain to do business with. Why can't you just cheat people like everyone else? Stop trying to fix the world's problems. Settle back with a girl and a bottle. You'll be much happier."

"Maybe, Vinny, but I don't think that's me."

We hung up and I called Tommy. He was looking for a job where Gloria's dazzling looks would not distract the boss or the customers. I knew it was not an easy task.

"Hey, Ryder. I thought I'd get back to you. I think I found a place for Gloria. I wish I could hire her, but I'd never be able to focus on my work, and the living men I deal with would be much too focused on her."

"She can't help it, Tommy. She hit the looks jackpot."

"That she did. Look don't ask how but I know a real interesting woman named Destiny Fairchild."

"That can't be her real name, Tommy."

"Nah, it isn't. At least I think it isn't. She's probably really Sally Jones. But she runs a small bar. Very fancy. For the well-off. Those that don't look at the prices on the menu. Anyway, I described you and Gloria.

"It turns out Destiny needs help. She says she had some of Gloria's problems when she was younger, and she's willing to give Gloria a chance. Only she wants to meet with you first."

Tommy gave me the bar's address and I promised to go over that afternoon.

I had some food and tried to think about what I'd

do to Claude Martine.

After eating I headed over to see what someone named Destiny Fairchild looked like.

It turned out that she looked like an angel. Her face was not one I had ever seen in a bar owner. Her flesh was ivory. Her eyes, the green of a summer field. Her hair a curly light brown that angels would have killed to have.

"Miss Fairchild?"

She looked me over. Those green eyes had become shrewd.

"I have my own buyers, mister."

"And you're smart to have them. My name is Jack Ryder. My friend Tommy told me he had spoken to you."

"He said you had killed people."

"I don't put that on my list of accomplishments. Sometimes the world needs to be swept up."

"And you're the broom."

"The broom with a weapon."

Destiny Fairchild smiled.

I didn't think she could be more beautiful until I saw that smile.

"Tommy said your wife died a couple of years ago."

"Sadly, she did."

"I'm sorry, Ryder. I really am. Tommy was the one who said I should call you Ryder. Is that okay?"

"Sure."

"Why do you want to give this woman Gloria a job?"

"Her former boss wanted her favors. On a weekly basis."

"That doesn't sound like it's any of your business."

"I like Gloria. That's how men treat her. I don't think it's fair. She thinks that's all she's worth."

"You very friendly with her?"

I stared hard at Destiny Fairchild.

"Not in the way you mean."

"You're a strange man."

"That is a fair assessment."

"You a private detective like Tommy said?"

"I call myself a fixer but it's the same job. I'm a private eye, a detective. Whatever you want to call it."

"That's a difficult job."

"Sometimes. Mostly I pick the jobs I want and help people"

"Tommy said it wasn't enough for you to help Gloria. I can work with you on that. But you're going to go after the boss who mistreated her."

"That's a possibility."

Destiny smiled again.

"I'd like to assist you. It is a small way for me to get back at men who did this to me."

"You don't want to do that. We're talking about some tough criminals. I might get hurt. I would not want you to get hurt. They'd go after your face. It's a nice one as it is."

"Thanks. I got it from my mother. My father's face looks like the south side of a horse heading north."

I couldn't help it. I smiled. My smile had nothing on Destiny's.

"So what do you say, Ryder? Do I get in on the fun?"

"I could use your help, but maybe in ways you wouldn't like."

"Such as using my looks."

"Exactly."

"I've been using my looks on men since I was about eleven. At least that's when I first became conscious of it.

We all use what we've got."

"I don't like using a woman's looks. I did it with Gloria, and I felt very guilty about it."

"We're two grown-ups talking, Ryder. When can we do it? I'm off this evening."

"Then this evening. We'll go have dinner there."

"Does this count as our first date?"

"It doesn't count as a date if we could both end up being beaten up."

"I've had worse first dates."

"I'll come by and get you at six. I hate myself for saying this, but wear something that the owner will think you a person worth conquering."

"My, Mr. Ryder, you will make a most interesting first date."

CHAPTER TWENTY-ONE

I worked my way through three cups of coffee. I had a fourth one, but it just sat there as I worked out what I wanted to say or do.

Satisfied, I first called Maxie.

"It's been too long, Ryder. People ask me about you all the time."

"Yeah. They ask how they can get rid of me."

"Nah. They like you. Sometimes. If you're calling me, you need something Ryder. Time is money. What do you want and how much will you give me?"

"I want to threaten Claude Martine. It's a personal matter. I want to tell him you've decided not to sell him any more meat."

"But I wouldn't do that, Ryder."

"Of course not. I just want to tell him."

"Watch what you say. I don't want to lose any business. I don't want him angry at me."

"Done. You get two hundred."

"Sorry, Ryder. There must be something wrong with the phone. I swear I heard you say two hundred which would be an insult to Maxie."

"Get your ears cleaned. I said four hundred."

"Done. As long as it ends up with me not losing the business. If so, you're going to cover the loss."

"Agreed."

Then it was time to speak with Detective Hill.

"Absolutely not," he said when I finished explaining what I wanted him to do. "I could get fired."

"It's for Gloria, not for me, Detective. And I'll owe you."

"What exactly can you do for me?"

"Make you feel better because you're helping someone and maybe stopping someone from taking advantage of young women."

"That, my friend, is a losing battle."

"So was the Alamo. But it was still worth fighting."

"You exhaust me, Ryder. Are you sure you didn't go to law school? All right. Not for you, but for Gloria and the women like her."

"And the two men?"

"Yes. I take it you'll get them from Vinny. Just make sure they're not killers."

"I'm after looks not killers."

"Remind me to look for other friends."

We talked some more and then I was back to thinking.

It was time to call Vinny. I described the two men I wanted. We agreed on a price, but he made it free when I told him it was for Gloria.

"I'll say it again. You're getting soft, Vinny."

"Don't let it get around, Ryder. My reputation counts for a lot in this business."

We hung up.

I thought I was set.

I went to Destiny Fairchild's bar.

"You look very attractive," I said.

"You're so loose with your compliments, Ryder. If I undid another button on my blouse I'd technically be arrested for stripping. But Martine's eyes will grow wide. He may even drool."

"That's the idea," I said.

I didn't tell Destiny the plan. I wanted her reactions to be spontaneous.

We went to Claude Martine's. I had made the reservation, and I was glad I did. It was crowded. The wealthy, who made money from the War and kept their sons out of it, drank to celebrate each other's importance in life.

A waitress came over to take our orders.

I checked my watch and nodded. As she was supposed to, Destiny called the waitress over, handed her a twenty dollar bill, and asked to speak to Mr. Martine about a personal matter.

The waitress pocketed the money, smiled, and left.

"Now, he's got to come," Destiny said.

"Oh he will. The waitress will describe you, and he'll break a few dishes in his mad dash to meet you."

"Why Mr. Ryder, I do believe you're doing a bit of flirting."

"I'm doing a bit of revenge."

"But you do find me attractive, right?"

Martine came over before I could answer.

He stood right next to Destiny.

I checked my watch and stretched out my hands. Destiny had to keep him occupied.

"I always come running when a beautiful woman calls."

"You'll get tired that way."

He laughed. It was an empty, tinny, false laugh.

"How may I help you and your husband?"

"Oh, this gentleman is not my husband. He's not my type. You are, Mr. Martine."

I think he blushed.

"And I'd like to prove I'm your type. What will it

take?"

I checked my watch and nodded.

"All you have to do is listen to this gentleman. If you agree with what he says, I think you and I can make a suitable arrangement."

He wasn't happy to leave her side, but Martine came over to me.

"I'm listening sir."

"Mr. Claude Martine, I'd like you to look at the front door."

The timing wasn't perfect but considering the circumstances it was very close.

Detective Hill, two of Vinny's men dressed up as cops, and Gloria came into the restaurant and walked up to us. Hill was there in case Martine asked to see a badge. The two men from Vinny were indistinguishable from escaped and hungry gorillas.

They stood there as I continued speaking.

I faced Martine.

"You fired this woman, Martine," I said pointing to Gloria. "And you fired her when she didn't agree to your demands. This woman is a very close friend of mine. So I have two messages for you. The first is from Maxie. He's no longer delivering meats to you."

"He wouldn't do that."

"I suggest you call him and tell him Ryder said the meats were gone."

"What's the other message?"

"This detective and these police are here to arrest you for receiving stolen meat. They will check your kitchen. Who knows? There may be other irregularities."

Martine looked at all of us. Destiny suddenly didn't look so attractive. I could see it on his face.

"Surely we can reach some agreement."

I paused, pretending to think over his offer.

"You apologize to Gloria. Give her a thousand dollars in cash. Promise her you won't bother other women employees. I'm going to mention that to our waitress."

"And Maxie keeps delivering meat?"

"Yes."

"Let me go get the money."

"One of the police officers will accompany you. I wouldn't want you going out the back door or bringing back a weapon."

Martine nodded.

The two men went.

Gloria bent down.

"Oh Mr. Ryder. A thousand dollars. You're amazing."

"Yes, he is," Destiny said. "And you look very nice tonight, Gloria. We're set for Thursday?"

"I'll be there Miss Fairchild."

"Without conditions," I said.

"Yes," Destiny said, "She doesn't have to be friendly to customers unless she wants to be."

Martine was back. He counted out ten one hundred dollar bills.

"I'm very sorry, Miss. I acted inappropriately. Please accept my apology."

I didn't think he sounded very sincere, but Gloria missed the subtlety and was clearly happy with what had happened. She put the money in her purse.

Hill, who hadn't said a word, walked out with Vinny's men.

Destiny and I got up. I signaled the waitress.

"We can't stay."

I handed her one of my cards.

"If Mr. Martine asks you to do anything you don't want to, please call me. I'll straighten him out."

Her mouth opened.

Destiny and I went back to her bar. She had her cook make us two hamburgers.

A hamburger never tasted so good.

CHAPTER TWENTY-TWO

"I'll walk you home," she said. "The evening air is so filled with dust and smoke that I'll just fade into being a part of New York City."

I looked at her.

"You're a very unusual person. In the best possible way."

She half bowed.

We went outside. There were fewer people on the streets than I expected.

One of the streetlights was out.

Destiny pointed at it and I said, "The city has darkened itself for us."

Just then a man behind me rushed up and put his very strong arm around my throat. I didn't see the other man coming. He emerged from a storefront's shadows. A third man dragged Destiny. All of us were in the shadows now.

The man who had been in the storefront's shadows stepped forward and said to me, "Mr. Ryder, you are not very good at taking messages."

Then he punched me in the stomach. Hard. I bent over. He stomped on my left foot. That got me to raise my head. Another punch to my throat. I was having trouble breathing.

"Don't move or the woman will get some of this."

I wasn't sure I could move if I wanted to, but I nodded. Two cars drove by. Neither one was filled with rescuers."

The man who had punched me leaned forward. We were almost nose to nose.

"I don't want to kill you, Ryder. Oh, your life means nothing to me. Understand that. Only I don't want police you know or gangsters for that matter looking for me."

He put his hand on my shoulder.

"It would not be gallant, but I can demonstrate my complete lack of conscience by taking the woman into this store and ruining her face. Permanently. I suppose you would not like me to do that."

I shook my head. I had no doubts that he would do it.

"Good. Then we need to come to some understanding. Some nun came to see you. I have no idea what false name she used, but you need to understand this. She has the most powerful enemies in the world. I am going to kill her and her ugly bodyguard. If necessary I am going to kill you, the women in your diner, your friend standing next to you, and anyone else who gets in the way of my task. Have I made myself clear, Mr. Ryder?"

I cleared my throat. I thought I could speak again.

"You have."

"That is good. So here is what you are to do. Nothing. Don't speak to the nun again. Don't do whatever she asked you to do. Don't give her any money. Simply stop your efforts on her behalf. The alternative for you and your friends is unpleasant in the extreme. And, Mr. Ryder, I have been trained in extreme unpleasantness. I will ask you only once: Do you understand me?"

"Yes."

"Do you know who I am?"

"You go by the name Tristan."

I was surprised. He smiled.

"I only asked to see if the nun knew I was on her trail. And now you have told me."

He suddenly punched me in the stomach.

Then he went over to Destiny. He put his hand under her chin.

"I wonder what acid would look like poured over this skin."

Then he punched her in the stomach.

She almost collapsed.

"Drop her," Tristan said, and the man holding Destiny pushed her down to the ground.

Tristan kicked her.

Then he turned to me.

"This is me being gentle. You don't want to see me being vicious. I am quite good at it. Do you agree to stop, Mr. Ryder?"

I was pretty sure anything I agreed to would not bind my conscience from any specific behavior.

"I agree."

He gently tapped my cheek.

"Of course I don't believe you. But this is your final warning. I have tried to restrain myself. I won't any more. You like living. Miss Fairchild here likes looking pretty. She likes walking without a wheelchair. I suggest you re-member your agreement."

Another few punches and I was down on the ground next to Destiny.

Tristan bent down.

"We will save the world. For thousands of years, the Jews had a chance. And look around. Communists, bankers, corruption, dirt, crime. We will clean it all up. We will re-make the world. If we don't do it the whole world will fall apart. We will destroy America. You just watch.”

He was waiting for me to respond, but I didn't want to please him by arguing.

A black sedan pulled up. The men got in it and drove away. I couldn't see the plate number.

When they turned the corner, I tried, with some effort to crawl toward Destiny.

I got there. She looked up at me. I was hoping to see a look of angry defiance on her face. Instead, she looked horrified. What kind of man had she found?

I stood up and, slowly, helped her to her feet.

“What are you going to do on the second date, Ryder?”

“Maybe Coney Island would be safer.”

“I'm right around the corner. Come to my apartment, and I'll fix us both up.”

We looked like two wounded war survivors struggling toward a home and a chair.

Once inside her apartment, she told me to lie down on the couch.

I didn't refuse.

She made us some coffee, and put out cookies. Caffeine and sugar. She was trying to bring us back to life.

After we ate, she got a washcloth and cleaned my face. Tristan was good. There was no blood anywhere. As far as I could tell there were no broken bones.

I was suddenly overwhelmed with exhaustion.

“The bed is one room over,” she said.

“That's one room too far.” I meant that in more ways than one, but I didn't want to explain.

Instead of going to her bed, Destiny came to the couch and leaned next to my head. I moved over a bit.

"Gloria told me about you. I mean about your wife. I hope you're not upset."

"What did she say?"

"She said you wouldn't make love to her because you thought that by doing so you'd be disloyal to your late wife. I told her that's ridiculous. That mourning takes time but eventually it ends. That you can't spend the next forty or fifty years kicking all possible romantic possibilities out the door. I told Gloria you just hadn't met the right woman. Someone who would make sure you didn't feel disloyal to the memory of your wife but who also made you comfortable with a new romantic partner. You think I was right to tell Gloria that?"

She bent down and kissed me.

"Don't you think I could be that woman?"

I looked up into her perfect face. Her eyes held compassion, not calculation. Her mouth was hungry for love not hungry to conquer a man.

"My mind is tired and covered with a blanket of confusion."

She nodded.

"Let's walk together through the fog."

She stood up and invited me to stand.

I did.

She took my hand.

"I'm not ready yet, Destiny. I'm going to go home. I apologize for what happened this evening. I apologize that I'm not the man you thought I was. I don't even know what kind of man I am."

"You are desperate to help others, Ryder, but you can't help yourself. You are a walking tragedy."

She walked me to the door.

I went out into the night. It had already betrayed

me once that evening. I feared it might happen again.

The streets were windier than usual. The smells were vivid.

I felt tired of my life.

CHAPTER TWENTY-THREE

The next day was warm. I didn't want to drive. I didn't want to walk. So I took a subway and went over to Park Avenue.

I had called and made an appointment with Walter Anderson, Kenny Benson's lawyer in what would have been a divorce case.

Park Avenue was crowded. People looked happier with their lives than did the people I ordinarily saw. The office was bright and big.

The secretary had a deep voice. Her fingernails had multi-colored butterflies on them.

"I'm here to see Mr. Anderson. My name is Ryder."

"Of course, Mr. Ryder."

She called into Anderson's office. Then she told me to go right in. That never happened to me. I always had to wait. And wait. Walter Anderson impressed me.

"You shouldn't call it a waiting room," I said. "You should call it a 'go right in' room."

She moved her lips in a valiant attempt to mimic a smile.

Anderson's office was as large as I expected. I wouldn't have wanted to be his window washer. There was a lot of window and it was high up.

Anderson himself evidently did not believe in denying himself food. He was Fatty Arbuckle without the scandal. At least I hoped so. He wore green suspenders. I thought for a minute and decided I had never

seen another human being wearing green suspenders. I
was glad I hadn't.

"Excuse me for not getting up, Mr. Ryder. If I did I'd
end up counting it as my exercise for the day."

Then he laughed.

I sat down in what was in the running for the most
comfortable chair in New York.

"Thank you very much for seeing me, Mr. Anderson."

"Kenny's is a sad case. I mean about his wife. You
said you were investigating the murder. That interested
me."

I nodded.

"I am doing so on behalf of the other victim in the
shooting, but of course I have to look at Della Benson as
well."

"I've made some calls about you, Mr. Ryder. It was
what people said that made me curious. I must say you
don't look much like a killer. Of course that would make
you a very good killer indeed, wouldn't it?"

"I didn't call about you, Mr. Anderson."

"Oh you should have. I'm known as the meanest divorce lawyer in the City. I'm not of course, but the reputation keeps my fees up so I never dispute it."

"How could Kenny Benson afford you? He's a soldier. They're not known for pulling down big salaries."

"I would have preferred some small talk, Mr. Ryder.
Maybe you would try some sweetness to calm me down,
get me off my game. Then I would have known you. But
being so direct? That's harder to figure out."

"I don't have time for anything but the truth."

"You'd have made a terrible lawyer."

"I notice, Mr. Anderson, that you didn't answer my

question."

"I know Mrs. Benson's lawyer. That is the gentle-man who was her lawyer before her demise. I hate him. He's beaten me in three straight cases. I took a ridicu-lously low fee from Mr. Benson, and he could barely afford that. But I wanted to prove that I could beat Rex Keller once and for all."

"Thank you. Although that was a long way around to answer one question."

Anderson was silent. He made a small tent of his fingers, waiting for me to continue.

"You have any suggestions about who might have wanted Della Benson dead? Besides yourself I mean."

"Now I see some of the killer in you. I didn't even know the woman. Why would I want her to die?"

I shrugged. "Killing her is one way to make sure Rex Keller couldn't beat you again."

"You are a nasty man in a nasty business, Mr. Ryder. I suddenly see that my schedule is too busy to continue speaking with you."

"So then who else might have wanted her dead?"

I thought he was going to swivel around in his chair and refuse to speak with me. Instead he puckered his lips.

"I thought your client was the other woman who was killed."

"It is, but I can't find anyone who could benefit from her death."

"You want a suspect besides me?"

"I'd appreciate it, Mr. Anderson."

"Fine. The man's name is Jesse Ryland. He was the man Della was having an affair with. He was the reason she wanted a divorce from a wounded soldier lying in his hospital bed in some godforsaken corner of Europe."

"But if Ryland loved her why would he kill her?"

"Yes I'm also amazed. Because no man who thought he was in love wanted to get rid of a clinging woman he had grown to hate. If he married her he'd be responsible for her."

Anderson's face was turning red.

"You have any money?"

"For useful information."

"Give me a hundred dollars. If you don't like the information, I'll give you the money back."

"In my world lawyers are not the single most trustworthy group of people."

"Gamble on me. I know stuff."

I handed him a hundred dollar bill.

"Dear sweet Della Benson was not the most loyal wife in the country. Jesse Ryland was not the first man she spent her evenings with."

"That's promising. I'm listening. There better be more."

"Oh, there's more. One of the men she spent time with got her pregnant."

"She wasn't pregnant at the time of her death."

"You are well-informed, Mr. Ryder. I'm impressed. She had the baby. It was a girl who lived with Della's sister. You'd think one pregnancy might at least have slowed Della down. Oh, no. More men followed. Then she got to dear Jesse. What a shock. Evidently Della had a special knack to get men to do what she wanted after she did what they wanted."

He stopped, pulled open a drawer from his desk, took out a glass and a bottle of whiskey. He didn't offer me a glass and I didn't ask for one. He had a drink. Then he replaced the glass and the bottle.

"Della got Jesse to ask her to marry him as soon as the divorce came through. He is a bit naïve as I'm sure you've already guessed. It was only then that she told him she had a kid not by Kenny, that she owed big money to her divorce lawyer, my friend Rex. And, oh yes, one other small matter. She told Jesse that she needed to continue seeing other men after they got married. Not wanted to. She said she needed such company."

"How do you know all this?"

Anderson laughed.

"Jesse told me. He wanted me to demolish Della on the stand. He wanted the world to know what she was like."

"All right, Anderson, then why kill her?"

The lawyer shrugged.

"I think his hatred kept building up. I can tell you when he spoke to me he was already furious. I'd say it got worse."

Anderson leaned forward.

"So, did I earn my hundred dollars?"

"You did."

"If Ryland has money, tell him I can represent him. It's no longer a divorce case, but the publicity will be fabulous for business."

"And if he doesn't have any money?"

"Forget my name."

"That's a deal Mr. Anderson."

I went out, said a polite good-bye to his secretary and walked outside.

Suddenly the air on Park Avenue seemed filled with dirt and scandal.

CHAPTER TWENTY-FOUR

I was sitting having some steak and potatoes and trying to enjoy the food. Ruth had brought it over and was trying to be nice to me. That meant she wanted more complex detective work to do. I was torn between worrying about her and wanting to give her a chance.

The diner's door opened and Sister Grace and her bodyguard entered. He looked around. The couple that never spoke to each other was at the counter. The single man who always wore his hat while eating was also at the counter but perpendicular to the couple. Another couple were at a table. They believed in animated conversation. From what I could tell the conversation revolved around their son who was in the Marines. The words went back and forth between pride and fear. I silently wished the Marine well and watched as Sister Grace came over to my table.

Her face looked ashen. Her New York visit must have been difficult.

"May I sit, Mr. Ryder?"

"Of course. You look as though you need it."

She didn't answer but slowly lowered herself into the seat.

"Mr. Ryder, can you get me a glass of water?"

I feared she was overworked and consumed by worry. Perhaps her fundraising had not gone as well as she had hoped.

I got her the water.

"I said a prayer for you in church this morning, Mr. Ryder. I hope you don't mind."

"Say some prayers. Light some candles. I need all the help I can get."

I was surprised she didn't smile.

"How are you doing with the Lonigan case, Mr. Ryder?"

Her voice was weak.

"I'm doing well. I have suspects. I will get there. I'm more hopeful now than when I started."

She nodded. "I'm very grateful for all your efforts."

She took a long sip of the water I had brought over.

"Mr. Ryder, I have a confession."

"I'm listening, Sister Grace. But I'm not sure I'm exactly the right person to hear your confession."

"Oh, but you are. Because besides the confession I need your help."

I leaned forward.

"Sister Grace, are you all right?"

"I...I couldn't tell you on my last visit, Mr. Ryder. I thought you would dismiss my plea for help. I'm dying. Cancer. If I didn't know better, I'd say the Nazis have somehow infected me. But they didn't. It is biology that is my enemy."

"I'm obviously very sorry."

She nodded.

"You're kind not to ask if it is fatal. It is. I have a few more months. So much to do. It is cruel of fate to let me die without seeing the Nazis defeated. Without seeing my children saved. It is more pain than what the cancer gives me. It is more pain than I can bear."

"Tell me how I can help you, Sister Grace."

Ruth came over and brought some food for Sister

Grace. Then Ruth sat down at the next booth.

"It's Tristan. He's captured six children and two of my workers. He didn't kill them immediately. He arranged for someone to tell me where the children are being held."

"He wants to lure you there."

"Most certainly. So he can kill me."

"Where is it? I'll try to save them."

"That's what I expected from you Mr. Ryder. They are being held on the eastern end of Long Island. They will be taken out of the country on a submarine that comes for them. This I have heard from contacts in Germany."

"Do you know where on Long Island? I mean the exact address."

"Yes. It is in Amagansett." She told me the street address. "The German submarine U-202 will pick them up in five days."

"Then let me round up some nasty boys and see what I can do."

She shook her head. "You do not know Tristan."

"I have in fact met him, Sister Grace. More exactly I met his fists and his threats."

Her mouth opened.

"I have put your life in danger."

"What use do I have for a life if I can't do good with it, Sister Grace?"

She was silent for fifteen seconds.

"I can't tell you how much I admire you, Mr. Ryder."

"We'll form a mutual admiration society."

"It won't do us any good. You'll surround the house with some, no offense, thugs that you know. And Tristan will say he wants to talk to me or the children. I can't bring myself to say what he'll do with the children unless I show up in person. The house will be one giant trap for anyone who wishes to enter. No. I have to go. I need help arranging a trade. My life for the children and my workers."

I looked down.

"Don't be sad, Mr. Ryder. Tristan doesn't know I'm dying. It will save months of pain. I will save the children. What's one life compared to that? Others will follow me. The Americans will come to Europe and save the people there. I cry that I won't be there to see it."

"Then what do you want me to do?"

"Get some of your best thugs and come with me. Let me give myself up. You must take care of the children. My bodyguard will tell you where to take them."

She told me where and when to meet her. She asked for five men besides me and two cars to take us out east.

"Don't look so sad, Mr. Ryder. The Lord has been good to me. He has given me a task. It is a waste not to have such a task. But I was given one and I did my best to complete it. A rabbi friend once quoted the Talmud to me. I don't remember it exactly but it was something to the effect that it was not our job to complete our mission, but to do whatever we can and go as far as we can."

"You're certainly doing that."

With that, Sister Grace got up and left the diner. She smiled at Ruth. It was a weak smile.

I watched as she and the bodyguard walked out the door.

Ruth came over and sat down.

"I did something I wasn't supposed to do, Mr. Ryder."

"What's that, Ruth?"

"I was eavesdropping. I heard what the nun said. I want to go along to save those children."

"Ruth, it's going to be dangerous."

"And that's why I need to go. You've been promising me that I'd get a chance to be a real detective. This is a chance to do that. Mr. Ryder, it's about saving children."

"I'm sorry, Ruth. I can't do it."

"Mr. Ryder, I deserve a chance to fight in this war. I deserve a chance to punch the Nazis for killing my husband. I deserve to grow up. I will stay back. I won't go charging into the house with a gun blazing."

"No guns. Positively."

"Okay. No guns. But give me a chance to be there. Please. I beg you."

I wasn't happy, but I nodded slowly.

She put her arms around my neck and kissed me on my cheek.

"I'm ready, Mr. Ryder. You'll see."

CHAPTER TWENTY-FIVE

The phone rang. It was ten-thirty in the morning so this wasn't much of a surprise. But it was a shock to my sleeping system. I'm often up for hours in the middle of the night but for some reason I sleep well during the hours when most people are getting up and starting their day.

I got to the phone and lifted it off the receiver.

I think I sounded like a wounded grizzly bear.

"Yeah?"

The sweet voice, awake and aware, came back to me.

"Mr. Ryder, you have to find out if this Nazi Tristan ever personally met Sister Grace."

I liked Ruth. I really did. But just at that moment I felt an overwhelming urge to slam the phone down. Hard.

"I asked her, Ruth. They've never met."

"And Tommy must employ make-up girls at his funeral home."

I admit the circumstances of the call were such that I couldn't quite grasp what Ruth was talking about. I kept thinking about the lure of losing consciousness.

I grunted.

"Don't you see, Mr. Ryder? I have a whole plan. Can I come over to see you? I don't want to say it on the phone."

I pictured sweet sleep moving further and further

from me. I had a fantasy of chasing it down the road but it kept moving further and further away as I ran.

"Come over if you have to, Ruth."

"I'm just on the corner. I'll be right there."

"Great."

I stumbled a bit as I got dressed and began to make coffee. The doorbell rang.

I had figured out what Ruth wanted, and I wasn't happy. I got the door.

How could she look so awake?

"Good morning, Mr. Ryder."

She held out a bag of cookies. I grabbed them. It would be a battle of sugar versus sleep.

I nodded. That took most of the rest of my strength.

We sat down.

"No," I said. "You can't."

"No? What do you mean?"

"You want to dress up like Sister Grace and confront Tristan. He's a literal monster, Ruth. He's a trained killer. You're good, but he spots those who don't belong in a minute. He's as ruthless as a human being can be. And he is desperate to kill Sister Grace and please his Nazi masters in Berlin."

"That focus is part of the plan. It could work. He'll have his entire focus on the rewards for finishing his mission. His mind will make me look like Sister Grace. And add makeup to make me look old. A pillow strapped to my stomach. A nun's outfit. How would he know?"

"I'd know."

She ignored me.

"But that's only half the plan, Mr. Ryder."

I took a few sips of coffee. I was almost back to

being a human.

I held up my hand to indicate that she should wait. A few more sips and then I nodded.

Ruth continued. "She's too important to risk her life. She can raise the money. She's the symbol for the whole effort. But I have a way to change the whole plan."

"And what's that, Ruth?"

She told me.

I sat and listened. I was a bit shocked that Ruth was capable of such planning. I knew she was smart, but I didn't know she was daring.

I hated to admit it, but it was an interesting plan.

"It's too dangerous, Ruth."

"You'll be there Mr. Ryder. And Vinny's men will be there. If Sister Grace goes in that house Tristan might shoot her right off. He might shoot the children. We need an alternate way of dealing with him."

"I have to check with Vinny if he could do it. I confess I'm proud of you, Ruth."

"I'm old enough to make the decisions that affect my life, Mr. Ryder. I'm old enough to fight in this war. I'm old enough to face a Nazi. Yes, to face death. I know that. But maybe, just maybe we can do this."

"Your plan is very high risk, Ruth. I have to admit I'm surprised you came up with it, Ruth. It's shocking."

"The war is very high risk. Life is very high risk."

I hated the fact that the idea was good. Sister Grace would want to face Tristan herself, but for better or worse I was now in charge of this. A sleepy armchair general. Just what the War needed. Just what captured Jewish children needed.

"Let me think about it, Ruth."

"We don't have time. And thinking about it is a

waste of time and is too often used as a polite way to say you won't do it."

I called Vinny. I told him what I needed. We could, I said, use the same trucks we used for the Queens warehouse. And Vinny always had men itching for a fight.

I asked Vinny about the special man we needed.

I thought he'd just say no. Or laugh at me.

"I know the guy for it. He lives in Jersey."

I had trapped myself. We could really do it. I decided not to call Sister Grace. If I did it, I didn't want her to even have a say. I knew she'd get angry. But the great among us do not have the right to get angry when we're trying to help them be great.

Ruth didn't know that Sister Grace was dying. I considered that. I decided that it would be a bad symbol if the Nazis killed her. It would be like they defeated the forces of good. Let her work until her dying breath. Let the possibility of a miracle hang in the air. From her sick bed she could inspire. From a Nazi grave she couldn't. From a grave of her own choosing she could.

I hated myself.

"All right, Ruth. A tentative yes. Talk to Tommy about make-up. Get a nun's habit. I'll have Vinny call you. You'll need to rehearse this."

I stared at her.

"Your uncle would kill me."

I put my hand on her shoulder.

"If you die, Ruth, I will never recover."

"And if I don't do this, Mr. Ryder, I will never really live."

We sat and talked.

I felt miserable because the more we talked the more sense Ruth made.

Finally, I checked my watch.

"I have a meeting, Ruth."

"Who with?"

"Della Benson's boyfriend."

"Wasn't she married to that guy in a hospital over-seas?"

"She was."

"It's too strange a world for a girl like me, Mr. Ryder."

"I think today we have to say you're a woman and not a girl."

Ruth nodded.

"Yeah. I like that. I guess I am."

CHAPTER TWENTY-SIX

I expected James Ryland to be smug, handsome and aware of it, well-off without being rich, and delighted to hear himself speaking.

When I walked into the restaurant to meet him, I looked around and didn't see the sort of man I expected. I asked if he had arrived.

A waiter led me to the table. No. Wrong man. This guy was older. I could see a handsome past hiding in his face, but it had escaped long ago and had gone far away. He didn't dress any better than I did, which is not a compliment. His left hand shook a bit as he sat there.

Ryland looked up as I stood at the table. "Mr. Ryder?"

"I am."

We shook hands. Maybe I had mistakenly come to a business meeting.

We sat.

The waiter took our orders. Ryland ordered a chicken salad sandwich. I ordered a well-done hamburger. The waiter didn't look too happy with either one of us.

When the waiter left, Ryland leaned forward and said, "I was surprised by your call, Mr. Ryder. Della Benson and I were connected in another lifetime. I'm not sure how I can help you. Oh, believe me, I would if I could. As long as the killer isn't found, some people will point at me. It's in my best interest to help and so here I am."

The voice was soft, sincere, and serious. He was either an accomplished actor or I was wasting a lunch. I should return my detective badge. If I had one.

"I am just trying to get some background information."

Ryland stared at me for a few seconds.

"You said you were a private detective who calls himself a fixer. I am a bookseller who calls himself confused. You surely don't think I have any connection to Della's unfortunate murder. I'm an innocent bystander in all of this. Am I in fact a suspect to you?"

"I'm just practicing the fundamentals of detection. Learn all you can about the victims. Go back to childhood if you can. That learning definitely includes men with whom she had a romantic relationship."

"It wasn't romantic. It was strictly physical. It was more precisely a business relationship. You want to hear about it, so I'll tell you. Yes, she was married. Yes, I knew it. Yes, it bothered me. I was single at the time. Actually I still am. She was a tigress on the hunt. She wanted a man. It was going to be me or someone else. I honestly don't think the man mattered too much to her."

"You said you sold books."

"And still do. She came in one day. I deal with some rare books I keep in a locked cabinet. But most people can't afford them. She couldn't either. But I told her I had first editions of all of Jane Austen's works. That may sound like an odd love call. But she changed when I said it. It was

like my arm was a magnet and her fingers were filings. They went right to me.

"She asked me to show her the books. Her very attractive eyes were opened wide. Blue the color of the

Pacific at Big Sur in California. The eyes hypnotized me. I showed her the books. She was surprised at the price. She…this is embarrassing, Mr. Ryder. Can I leave it that she offered to pay me for the book using an alternate currency?"

"I get the idea, Mr. Ryland."

"I have to say. I didn't see her as an avid book collector. Frankly, I was surprised she would care to read Jane Austen. I would have said she read books aimed at women seeking romance but books without any literary merit. At any rate, I offered her the cheapest book. I admit it. I wasn't thinking right. My whole body felt taken over by desire. I feel more than a little shame as I confess. Are you going to make me say a hundred Hail Marys?"

"I'm no priest, Mr. Ryland. I'm very far from a priest."

"That is a relief. The pay-off for the book was our relationship. Once a week. I paid for a meal and an hour at a hotel she knew about. Week by week she paid for the book. I'm reasonably sure Jane Austen would have been appalled. I wasn't exactly following a bookseller's ethic. But that was it. She gave me a bonus weekly session after she had finished paying. And then we parted as friends. We each had a story to tell. Another confession. I think about her sometimes. It is shameful to say, but I find the story pleasing as I re-tell it to myself."

He lowered his head.

"I've never done that with another customer, before or since."

"Were you angry with her?'

He made a big sigh.

"Why don't you just ask me? Never mind. I'll give

you the answer that you need. I read all about her murder. I was in the bookstore at the time. Many people saw me. One man in particular can provide me with an alibi. I have made a hobby of collecting Sinclair Lewis first editions. This gentleman had a first edition of *Main Street.* He offered it to me at a very reasonable price. I entered the date and time in my ledger. I made a check out to him. Oh, he trusted me. I had bought several other books from him."

Ryland shook his head. "Besides, Mr. Ryder, what reason on God's green earth would I have for harming Della Benson? I hadn't loved her. She hadn't loved me. We had separated. As far as I know she was either back with her husband or had found another bookseller with more Jane Austens. Maybe by now she has the whole collection. Or she has Dickens. The way she harpooned me, maybe she has a Melville."

He lowered his head and stared at me.

"Go ahead. Ask me any questions you have."

"Just the obvious one, Mr. Ryland. Is there anyone you know who might have had a motive to kill Mrs. Benson?"

"A spurned lover. Someone who wanted her but was rejected. I take it from the papers that Mr. Benson the cuckold in this drama was overseas at the time of the murder. I would have put him at the top of the list. In the crime stories I hear on the radio it's always the husband or wife. They're so dull and predictable. But other than that I have no ideas."

And neither did I.

CHAPTER TWENTY-SEVEN

Adam Lonigan called me the next morning. He asked me to come over to his place. He gave me some foreign coffee when I got there. I liked experimenting with different coffees, and, unsurprisingly, I liked the taste of this one.

"I got a call this morning Mr. Ryder, one you should know about."

I was unsure whether to tell him what I thought but the offer to tell me some news helped me put off a decision.

"I'm curious to hear it, Mr. Lonigan."

"Good. The call came from Kenny Benson. He came home two days ago. No fanfare. Radio silence he called it. He wanted to tell me how sorry he was to hear about my daughter. I expressed similar sympathies toward his wife. I take it you wish to speak with him, Mr. Ryder."

"I most definitely do."

Lonigan handed me a slip with the Benson address, which I already knew, and the phone number, which I did not.

"I'm not sure he has much to tell you."

"I guess I'll find out."

It was just then that I decided not to tell him that I knew who killed his daughter and why. Figuring out the killer was easy. But I didn't tell him because I had no evidence and it seemed simply cruel to tell a man you know who shot his child but you can't prove it so you can't send him to jail. I needed a confession and didn't think I could get it.

Lonigan was a nice man, and we talked about War news, sports, a movie he had seen, and worked very hard to avoid talking about the case.

I eventually left and took a cab to Destiny Fairchild's bar.

The place was dark and despite the relatively early hour it was pretty packed. Destiny saw me before I saw her.

She walked up to me and planted a kiss.

"Now never wash your cheek again, Ryder."

"I don't wash it all that often now."

We both smiled.

"Your girl Gloria is working out great, by the way."

"It was kind of you to offer her work."

"Are you kidding? I have her sit at the bar and time how long it takes for twenty men to walk up and offer her a drink. She said it would be more interesting if instead of asking what she wanted to drink they asked her for what they really wanted.

"It would save time, that's what she said."

"She just around to attract the boys?"

"Oh, no Ryder. I asked her what she wanted, and she said she wanted to develop her cooking skills, so she spends a lot of time in the kitchen. We're a hamburger place. Not a lot of sophisticated palates, but she practices. And she's good. She's got a lot of natural talent. I hired a more experienced cook and he's teaching her."

"You've earned your Girl Scout badges."

"I could have been her, and she could have been me. I'm not kidding myself."

"Maybe I should go into the kitchen and say hello."

"Gloria would like that very much. Who knows how many free hamburgers she'll offer you? But before you do that, I want to sit at a table with you and talk."

I looked around.

"We'll take a spot from customers."

"I don't mean out here. I mean in my private office."

I looked at her face in a different way. Five years had crept onto it. Wisdom had congealed in her eyes.

I nodded, and then I followed her. The bar was mahogany all over. It smelled of liquor and desires of all kinds.

Her office was well-lit and had a smell of a very pleasant perfume.

"You do the decoration?"

"I'm surprised you ask Ryder, but yes I did." She paused and then said, "Come and sit on the couch."

She walked over and sat down. I sat next to her. I didn't lean in to kiss her. She looked as though she didn't want me to do so.

"I'll remember you. Later, I'll have arguments with my husband, run to another room, or send him off to a bed in the basement or a hotel. And I'll sit there. You might think I'd be nursing a drink or two. Add a pound a week to my ever-expanding body. Spend a lot of wasted time crying. Have to give away all my old clothes. Have to give away all my old hopes."

Destiny gave me a wistful smile and leaned back.

"But you'd be wrong, Ryder. I would think of you. I'll think of you as the man that got away. Of course that will be a cloud of self-delusion. You're not the one who got away. You're the one who never wanted to find a home in my arms."

"You're right and you're wrong, Destiny."

"Thanks for the clarity."

"My moral code stands guard against my desire."

"Ah, the Ryder code. You should burn it. Have a ceremony. I'll bring the drinks. And after you burn this prison that you call a moral code we can have a good time."

"Maybe you're right, Destiny. But maybe you're wrong. I am who I am."

"I brought you in here to tell you about another character who is about to enter the conversation. His name doesn't matter. But he and I have known each other for a while. I didn't think of him as a romantic partner. He always thought of me as one."

"And you had a sudden insight that he's the right man."

"You're not only puzzling, Ryder. You're cruel. We're trying it out. I think it will work. I'm older. And now I'm tired. I can see in your face that you would lead me down a road that is sad and lonely. The very road where you've led yourself. It's not that I wouldn't go with you. I don't even know. It's that you wouldn't let me go with you. I pity you, Ryder. I really do."

"This is a painful way to say good-bye, Destiny."

"Oh, it's not good-bye. You can come in here whenever you want. Say hi to Gloria. Say hi to me if it's not too painful to do so. But this is good-bye to us."

I didn't know what to do or say. Instead I stood up and walked out of the office. I stopped at the door, though, and looked back at her. Destiny was looking down, heroically struggling to hold back any tears of regret.

I stopped off for five minutes in the kitchen. Gloria was busy, though. The new cook Destiny had hired was a handsome man, and Gloria paid attention to him as though he were an oracle.

I walked out into the late afternoon sun. There were clouds floating toward me.

I went over to 75 ½ Barrow Street to the narrowest house in Greenwich Village. It is only nine and a half feet wide. It was built in 1873. I stared at it and thought its literary inhabitants might have seen it as a grave from which they emerged each day.

Edna St. Vincent Millay had once lived there. The house had three stories with an odd gable. Millay had lived there from 1923 to 1924. Millay was the new woman, the new person really, who, in the years after the First World War, concluded that all the restrictions of the past had to be thrown off. The past had to be discarded. She wrote of a candle burning from both ends. I felt that way about my life. It was burning from both ends and a blowtorch was then put to the middle of the candle.

My feet felt on fire as I kept walking. Maybe if I didn't have a job to do I would have never stopped walking.

But I did have a job. I had to figure out how I was going to speak with Kenny Benson.

CHAPTER TWENTY-EIGHT

I called Kenny Benson early the next morning, at least early for me. I told him I was working for Adam Lonigan, the father of the woman Della had been with when she got shot.

"I'm not in the best shape, mister. I get real tired. And now I'm real lonely."

"I appreciate that Mr. Benson. It will only take a few minutes and I want to thank you in person for what you have done for our country. I need to tell Mr. Lonigan that I spoke to everyone, so you'd be doing me a big favor."

"Just a few minutes."

"That's right. Then I can wrap up my investigation."

"All right. Can you be here at three?"

"Sure."

We hung up and then I called Detective Simon Hill. I asked him to come with me and told him what I wanted. He agreed.

We arrived at Benson's apartment five minutes early. I heard him coughing. There was a trail of the coughing as he approached the door to let us inside.

The coughing stopped as he opened the door.

"Hello," I said. "I'm Jack Ryder. I called you earlier."

"I got shot in the chest, not the brain. I remember you. Who's this with you?"

"This is a friend, Simon Hill. We're going to his

place after we leave here. He can stay outside if you don't want him to come in."

"No. It's all right. He looks like he'd appreciate a veteran."

"I would and do," Hill said.

We walked in. The apartment was plain and functional. Simple chairs.

I coughed. Then I did so again.

"Sorry, Mr. Benson. I got a frog in my throat. I hate to ask it right off but can I have something to drink?"

"You can have a beer. You too Mr. Hill?"

"No thanks," he said. "I like to shoot the frogs not drown 'em."

Benson liked that. He got up, went to the refrigerator and got me a can of beer.

I hate beer. I hate its smell. I hate its taste. But I took a long sip, made a sound of satisfaction and thanked Benson.

When I was done, I said, "I wasn't kidding before. Hill and I were just saying as we came here it's great to meet a real hero, someone willing to take a bullet for our country."

"Yeah, well I took three bullets. Three burning bullets that beat me up pretty bad. Only decent part was the nurses. Some of them were real pretty."

"A pretty nurse takes away a lot of pain," I said.

Benson nodded.

Then he said, "You got two minutes Ryder. What can I possibly say about Della's death and the death of the woman you care about?"

"Oh, Mr. Benson, I care about both. I came here to tell you I know who killed Miss Lonigan as well as your wife."

Benson's eyes narrowed.

"The police haven't told me that."

"They're just learning it."

"Yeah? So who did it?"

"Why you did, Mr. Benson."

He paused. He stared at me. And then he laughed.

"What are you talking about? I was lying in a hospital bed barely able to move when Della got shot."

"I know where you were, Mr. Benson, but I know you ordered the killing."

"Who did I call? Al Capone's old gang?"

"You called your friend Markie Fuller." I paused to check my watch. "Indeed, I should tell you that the Village Police in Sag Harbor picked him up fifteen minutes ago and are charging him with two counts of murder and one count of attempted murder. I imagine he's singing like Bing Crosby, trying to save himself from a trip to a small room in Sing Sing where they fry people."

"I don't believe you, Ryder."

I shrugged. "Before we go any further, I need to more formally introduce my friend Mr. Hill here. He's Detective Simon Hill. He's in the Homicide Division in the New York City police department."

"He looks it. But I don't believe the rest of it."

"Oh, I knew Mr. Fuller was guilty as soon as I left his house in Sag Harbor. I had to go on with my investigation to cover all the possibilities, but I knew. Shall I tell you how I knew?"

"Yeah. Sure. That's probably a lie too."

I smiled a little.

"It's not a lie. When I came in here I asked for a drink. You were a good host and got me one. When I was at Fuller's house I asked for a drink, but Fuller didn't get up. He called for Faith, his wife, to get us some lemonade."

"So what does that prove?"

"To me, a lot, Benson. There was a witness to the murders. Benny, the guy who owned the bakery. Benny is a sharp guy. Like you he wasn't shot in the brain either. He saw that the shooter had a limp. That's why Fuller didn't get up. He didn't want to show us the limp."

"That ain't much. Good luck in court with a guy with a limp."

"Oh that's not all, Mr. Benson. As I said, Benny is very sharp. I made a recording of Mr. Fuller when I was there. I took the recording to an expert in the police department in charge of taped confessions. He was a guy who could make it sound very clear. Then I brought Benny in and played it and Benny said yeah he was sure Fuller's was the voice of the shooter."

I leaned back and stretched out my legs. "The cops are going to tell Fuller they're gonna charge his wife as the accomplice in the shooting."

"She didn't have nothing to do with it."

"Oh, we know that Mr. Benson. You and I know what happened. But the cops, they're out there away from the City. They'll take the easy way out unless I can tell them another story. With proof. Or a confession. They'll threaten his wife until he gives you up, Mr. Benson. What's your bet? My money is on three minutes."

Benson was sweating now.

I tilted my head to one side and said, "You want me to tell you what happened? That might make it easier for you."

Benson was silent. I pushed forward before I lost him.

"You're lying in the hospital bed, maybe thinking of a pretty nurse, maybe thinking of your wife, maybe going back and forth between the two. And then it's mail call. And, lucky you, you get a letter from Della. But the letter is a disaster. It's a Dear John letter. Sorry, buddy, but I found someone new. Good luck and all that but someone else is keeping me warm tonight."

"Shut up."

"And all you had to do all day was get more and more furious. You were like a prisoner. Revenge was all you could think about. I mean you had a perfect alibi. You didn't want to wait until you got home. By then who knows where Della and her new boyfriend would be hiding out? No, you had to strike fast.

"Luckily, Benson, you could. You knew somebody not far from New York with military training in firearms. Someone you could trust. Someone who would be a soldier and carry out the assignment without complaining. You and Fuller were great friends. Your heart poured out in the letters you wrote him and then, one day, you asked him. What did you say, Benson? Did you say it would be great if someone taught Della the biggest lesson you can learn in life? He'd get it. He knew your pain."

I turned silent.

It was Detective Hill's turn.

Hill cleared his throat.

"Mr. Benson, I don't know about any of this. But I can tell you the more you talk now, the more honest you are, the better off you'll be. For example, Mr. Ryder here is friends with one of the cops in Sag Harbor. You could do yourself a giant favor. Let's assume Faith Fuller wasn't her husband's accomplice. Tell us who was. You've got to do this fast. You have to beat Fuller to get full advantage from this. I've got nothing at stake. But you're a wounded vet. I'm on your side. My wife ever wrote me one of those letters, well, I always have my weapon by my side. I'd have used it, I can tell you that. So I understand you. I really do. I want to see you get a break. But if you sit there and don't say anything, or even worse you deny this, you're just making it worse for yourself."

"Della always liked the boys. I knew that when I married her. But I figured marriage would calm her down. She was real pretty. So that was the story I told myself."

I let Hill go at it.

Hill was almost whispering.

"Who was the other shooter, Kenny?"

"Fuller's little brother Teddy. Only he didn't shoot. He just stood there. Markie wouldn't let him shoot. Markie did all the shooting. He shot Della first. And then he wanted to get rid of witnesses. I guess he didn't do a good enough job with the bakery owner."

Benson looked first at Hill and then at me.

"You two see that she deserved it, right? She abandoned a soldier on the battlefield. She didn't just betray me. She betrayed the country. She deserved the death penalty. Right?"

"We're not a jury, Benson. Only I wouldn't count on their sympathy."

"So what happens now?"

"I take you in," Detective Hill said. "We go through this in the station. We take it all down. The District Attorney will have to figure out what to do with you guys."

"You think he'll understand?" Benson asked.

I stared at him. I was angry and annoyed.

"He may understand about Della Mr. Benson. He's

not going to understand about Miss Lonigan. She was a sweet and kind young woman. Her father had a heart attack when he learned she had died. She was his only child. The jury's not going to forget her."

"That's on Markie. I only told him to get Della."

We talked and argued some more and then Detective Hill took Kenny Benson to discover the first step in the justice system. Hill put Benson handcuffs on and put him into a car.

Then Hill came over to me. "What was that nonsense? He doesn't get up so you think he had a limp? No judge in the universe is going to accept that. And what in Heaven's name was that police unit about hearing taped confessions?"

"I sort of made it up."

"You didn't tape Fuller in Sag Harbor, did you?"

"I was too dumb to think of it."

"So you couldn't play this magical tape for Benny."

"He was too shook up to have been able to pick out a voice. He wasn't even sure about a limp."

"I can't tell my bosses that."

"Just tell them about the confession."

"You'd be fired if you were a cop and did that."

"I guess it's lucky for justice that I'm not a cop."

"It's lucky for everyone that you're not a cop."

Hill said he'd call the police in Sag Harbor and have Fuller and his brother arrested and grilled until confessions came out.

I watched Hill drive off with his prisoner.

Then I drove over to Adam Lonigan's house and told him the whole story. I told him we had the person who ordered the killing in custody and would soon have the shooter and his accomplice in jail. I left out Benson's side of the story. Lonigan wouldn't care.

"Mr. Lonigan, a deal is a deal. I expect you to call Sister Grace and make good on your promise."

"No offense, Mr. Ryder, but let me verify your story, and I'll be quick to do as I said. I told her and I told you I deeply admire her work."

We shook hands.

He looked at me and said, "Mr. Ryder you've saved my life and, I'm sure, the lives of many children. You have justified your existence. That's more than most people can say."

I nodded and left.

I had a few days to prepare to go to Amagansett to rescue the captured children.

CHAPTER TWENTY-NINE

Five men, along with Ruth, Sister Grace, and I were in three cars instead of the two Sister Grace had asked for. One of Vinny's men had decided at the last minute not to go with us. Vinny couldn't find a replacement. So he came himself.

The man Ruth had requested, the one from New Jersey, was in the back. He and Ruth had spent an hour practicing and getting used to each other. His name was Hank and let's just say Ruth was a very brave woman.

We drove solemnly east on Long Island roads. There was a silence that seemed palpable.

Vinny said to me, "You know, Ryder, he could just shoot us. You have any idea how many men he has with him?"

"No."

"You know what weapons they have?"

"No."

"It's possible they could have set land mines. We'll be killed just trying to walk into the house."

"I know, Vinny."

"And you think this Nazi pig is going to be fooled by Ruth dressed up as a nun like this is a school play?"

"We're going to do our best, Vinny."

With that, he lapsed into silence.

I got lost once driving and had to stop at a gas station for directions.

Then a cop pulled us over.

I stared into the interior of the car I was driving.

"You got two nuns in there," he said in astonishment.

"It's a religious retreat," I said.

"Those boys in the other car don't look so religious," the cop said.

"Who else is in need of a religious retreat, officer?" It was Sister Grace. She knew how to speak with the authority of someone mouthing God's thunderous voice.

"This ain't a pleasure trip is it?" The cop was still thoroughly confused.

"There's always pleasure in communing with God, officer." Sister Grace's voice, though still raspy, sounded serene and sweet.

"All right. You folks move on. Have a pleasant Long Island day."

We all thanked him and continued the journey. Amagansett is on the South Shore. You could smell the water and see the sand as you went.

We finally came to a stop a block away from the house. It stood alone. I had planned to have Vinny's men clear the neighbors out of their homes, but there would be no need for that.

"We'll walk to the house. Ruth, you and Hank get ready. I'll go with you. The other men wait outside ready to come in if they hear shots or me yelling.

"There's a Coast Guard station not far from here, Ryder," Vinny said. "Maybe we should call on them for help. They're supposed to look for Nazis. They even found some last year."

"We're the fighters here, Vinny. But it's good to know there is help around.

We started walking, going very slowly because of

Ruth and Hank.

We got to the front door.

I knocked loudly.

A man in full Nazi uniform answered.

"Just the nun," he said.

"She's not going anywhere unless I go too."

The Nazi grunted.

"I don't like your looks mister. You look like a Jew. You look at me the wrong way I'll shoot you. You make a sudden move I don't like, I'll shoot you."

"We're here to make a trade."

He let us in.

I knew that as soon as the door closed, the others in our group would move toward the house. Sister Grace would remain in the car.

The Nazi took us into the living room. It was plain, a summer house for a wealthy city dweller.

Tristan was standing in the middle of the room.

He made a half bow. He even made the bow look mocking.

"It is good to see you again, Ryder."

He turned and said, "And we meet at last, Sister Grace. You've been quite an annoyance to Herr Hitler. He really doesn't like you."

"I assure you the feeling flows in both directions," Ruth said. "I'm here for the deal."

"Yes, but I'm afraid I've gotten new instructions from Berlin. First we are to kill you. That will take a while. I'm afraid the Fuhrer wants you to feel the pain you have inflicted on him."

"You mean you intend to torture me."

"It would be ungentlemanly of me to describe exactly what is to be done, but if I were you I would prepare for an extended period of unpleasantness.”

“We will resist,” I said.

That was the signal to Hank.

Hank, a dwarf with the abilities of a professional killer, came out from under Ruth’s habit.

The Nazi had stepped in front of Tristan.

Hank shot him in the face, and he collapsed.

Two other Nazis came into the room.

Our men from outside rushed into the house.

There was a gun fight, but I was busy.

Tristan had run, and I ran after him. He wasn’t as fast as I expected.

I caught up to him, jumped on a couch, and leaped putting my hands out to grab him.

We tumbled on the ground.

I hadn’t seen the knife he was carrying in his right hand.

He lifted it high and I watched the blade as Tristan began to bring it down.

He didn’t get far.

Vinny shot him in the arm. The blood trickled out as he fell.

I leaned over him.

“My friend chose not to kill you. In fact he was careful not to kill you.”

I paused. “Whatever your real name is, I’m sure your superiors won’t be happy. But I’m not thinking of them at this minute. Instead, I have a hope. I hope God has a better imagination than I do. I can’t even come up with as bad a punishment as you deserve.”

He was holding his arm.

“Here is part of that punishment.”

I shot him between his eyes.

His head dropped. I checked for a pulse.

He was dead.

I rushed upstairs and found the children and the two of Sister Grace's co-workers tied up in one of the bedrooms.

Two of the children were crying.

I reached into my pocket and pulled out some of the candy I had brought. Gertie had told me to bring food, but I said there would be time enough for that. They would be in shock and chocolate is the greatest known medicine to beat shock.

This completely made-up point of view seemed right to me because the children gobbled the candy and asked for more.

I went downstairs and suddenly stopped.

Ruth had been shot.

I rushed over to her.

"Mr. Ryder. I've been wounded. The Nazis shot a nun."

I looked at her injury.

"It's a flesh wound, Ruth. It's bleeding. But there are no broken bones, no vital organs that have been hit. You'll be fine."

"Oh, no, Mr. Ryder. You're wrong. It's a big wound, big enough to brag about, big enough to make me a professional."

"And big enough not to talk about with your uncle."

We took the children in one of the captors' cars. Sister Grace guided us to a place in East Hampton where her bodyguard was waiting. The children and the co-workers would be safe. They would become great Americans.

They would have a story to tell someday after the
War ended.

CHAPTER THIRTY

Sister Grace and I were seated at the booth in the diner. It was late but not as late as it usually was when I was there. Gertie had put a "closed" sign on the front door. Sister Grace's bodyguard made sure no one ignored the sign and entered.

Ruth was shy about approaching us. She stood by the front counter.

"It's been a long journey since I first entered here," Sister Grace said.

"Mostly a successful journey."

"Yes, it has been Mr. Ryder. As he promised, Mr. Lonigan has donated his money. I saw him and for the first time he looked almost content. The children have been placed through a cooperative orphanage in homes around your country. I think our work in America to gain funds has gone extremely well. And that's mostly because of you, Mr. Ryder. I'm ready to nominate you for sainthood, but sadly I won't be around to be able to do so."

"What does your doctor say, Sister Grace?"

She laughed. I finally got a laugh out of her, though for the wrong reason.

"He says what he always says. I should slow down. When the Nazis slow down I'll go twice as hard just to beat them. I told my doctor I would slow down fifteen minutes after I die."

I didn't mention to her that she looked considerably worse each day that I saw her.

"You look as though you have a question, Mr. Ryder."

"I do, but I'm embarrassed to ask it."

"What? After all we've been through together? Go ahead. I'm a tough nun."

"That I know you are, Sister Grace. I wanted to know if you're scared of death. I mean with your religious faith."

"Faith makes us strong. It makes everyone strong. Except me. I'm scared. I think life is so important because of the good we can do. We can't do any good lying around in the earth. I don't want to waste space. I don't want to stop doing good. Yes, Mr. Ryder. I'm scared and disappointed that God has chosen to end this for me. Or rather that cancer has decided to appear. Couldn't it have waited ten years? By then we would have won this war. That would make death's sting less powerful. And what about you, Mr. Ryder?"

"I live in a state of confusion about it and about much else."

"That's all right. Stay confused as long as you keep helping people in the way that you do."

Sister Grace and I sipped our cups of coffee.

"I'll have someone contact you when I go, Mr. Ryder. I want you to know. I…I have one last favor to ask of you. It would make my exit from existence more bearable."

"Whatever you want, Sister Grace. Whatever."

"Thank you. I want you to do some good deeds in my name. That's the only way I can continue to live in the way that I want to. I can die in peace if I know you will help the children who are hurting. Help to remember the victims of violence and deceit and hatred. It pains me, as I told you, to watch the Jewish people being murdered and tortured for no reason other than who they are. Help them get through this war if you can. Help all the victims of this War. Help everyone in this world who needs it."

"There's not much I can do."

She nodded.

"Who knows what is around the corner for any of us Mr. Ryder?"

"A good motto for life."

Sister Grace stood up.

"And now I leave you, Mr. Ryder."

There was so much sadness in that statement that all I could do for a moment was be silent.

Then I said, "It's been one of the greatest honors of my life to meet you and to help you."

She nodded. "God has brought us together to do good, Mr. Ryder. And we have done it. May God bless you."

"And you as well Sister Grace."

I watched as she walked down the aisle, opened the door, and stepped out into the dark and dangerous world.

THE END

ABOUT THE AUTHOR

Lawrence J. Epstein

Lawrence J. Epstein served as an Advisor for two members of the United States Congress and two additional Congressional candidates. He is also a former English professor and the author of more than twenty books.

Please sign up for his mailing list to be among the first to know when his next Ryder novel will be published: http://www.lawrencejepstein.com/list

See his list of books on his Amazon Author Central Page: https://authorcentral.amazon.com/gp/books

You can contact the author at: lawrencejepstein@gmail.com.

Please consider leaving a review of this book on Amazon.com and Goodreads.com.

Thank you.